TEN FROM INFINITY

MORE WILDSIDE CLASSICS

TEN FROM INFINITY

PAUL W. FAIRMAN

(WRITING AS IVAR JORGENSEN)

WILDSIDE PRESS

TEN FROM INFINITY

1

It began when a pedestrian got hit by a cab at the corner of 59th Street and Park Avenue, Manhattan, New York City, U.S.A. No doubt it was the first motor mishap in the history of creation that reached out among the stars.

The pedestrian was walking south on Park Avenue, toward Grand Central Station. He was looking at the upper skeleton of the vast new Pan Am Building which blocked out the sky in that direction. But he should have been watching traffic because a yellow cab tagged him neatly and knocked him across the walk into a clump of pigeons that scattered upward in all directions.

The cab driver swore. Citizenry gathered. An alert free-lance news photographer who happened to be passing took the most important shot of his career. After a while, the ambulance came and the dazed pedestrian was pointed toward the nearest emergency ward, which happened to be in the Park Hill Hospital.

The pigeons settled back. The curious went their different ways.

And far out in space, among the yellow pinpoints we call stars, a signal was registered. The signal was of grave import to those who received it.

The signal said, *Something has gone wrong.*

*****

From the springboard of this incident, there emerged several occurrences of note. The first in sequence took place in the Park Hill Hospital. The time of that particular ambulance's arrival was 11:15 P.M. At that hour the harvest of violence in Manhattan was being delivered to its logical granaries in the form of broken heads, slashed bodies, and dazed, shock-strained eyes. The examining rooms at Park Hill were full, and some cases of lesser import were waiting on stretchers and benches in the corridors.

That was where the pedestrian waited. Unlike others, he was very patient. He seemed to understand that this sort of thing took time; or perhaps he didn't. At any rate, he lay staring up at the ceiling, unmoving, seemingly uncaring, until an intern named Frank Corson stopped beside his stretcher and looked down at him in moody-eyed weariness. Then Corson managed a smile.

"Sorry about the service, mister. Full house tonight."

"That's quite all—right."

Corson touched the broken leg. "I can give you a shot if the pain's hitting too hard."

"It does not—pain."

"Stout fellow." Frank Corson probed with fingers that were growing more expert day by day. "Good clean break. Not swelling, either." He touched the patient's wrist, then put a stethoscope to his chest.

Actually, he was thinking of a different chest and different legs at the time—the ones belonging to a copper-haired girl named Rhoda Kane. Rhoda's legs were far more alluring. Her chest had added equipment that was a haven of rest under trying circumstances, and Corson yearned for midnight when he would quit this charnel house and climb into Rhoda's convertible and—perhaps later—do a little chest analysis without benefit of stethoscope.

Now he sighed, commandeered a passing orderly, and went to work.

Twenty minutes later he saw his patient deposited in a ten-bed ward. He transcribed his data onto the clipboard at the foot of the bed, and looked guiltily into the hall to see how things were going. He felt guilty because he was tempted to dog it. And he did. He headed for the locker room where he punched a cup of coffee out of the machine and thought some more about Rhoda's legs.

Fifteen minutes later, Corson climbed into the convertible and leaned over and kissed Rhoda Kane. "Hi, baby. You smell wonderful."

"You smell of disinfectant, darling." She wore a yellow print dress that exposed a lot of healthily tanned skin. "Did you have a rough day?"

He leaned back against the seat and pushed his legs as far under the dashboard as possible. He sighed and closed his eyes. But then he opened them again and his face went blank.

She waited a few more moments and then said, "Honey—I'm here. Little Rhoda. Remember me?"

The vague, thoughtful look vanished as he jerked his head around. "Oh, sure—sure, baby." He grinned. "A rough one. If I'd known doctoring was like this I'd have been a nice prosperous butcher."

"Do you want to drive?"

"No, you drive. I'll sit here and look at your beautiful profile."

They drove to Rhoda's apartment—Frank couldn't afford one—and he put Rhoda at one end of the sofa and stretched out with his head in her lap. He unbuttoned her blouse, put a hand over her breast, and teased the nipple.

"Mr. Corson, you're a wolf."

"Kiss me."

"Well, I don't know," she teased.

He pulled her head down and she murmured, "Oh, darling. . . ."

But he let go of her in the middle of the kiss and, when she straightened, the blank, thoughtful look was back on his face.

"Frank—what is it?"

The look stayed. "I don't know."

"Something's bothering you."

"It seems to be. But I don't know what it is."

"Did it happen at the hospital?"

He frowned. "I guess it must have. It's been bugging me since—"

Rhoda showed concern. "Did it have to do with a patient?"

"Patients are all I work with. Let's see—" He stopped and his frown deepened. "It was that damned accident case. Broken leg. I set it and put him in ward five. I—"

His frown deepened as he sat up. "Uh-huh. It was that damned pulse. That's it. There was something wrong. That pulse was even and steady but, Goddamn it, something was wrong!" He got to his feet. "Baby—I've got to go back to Park Hill."

"Do you want to take the car or shall I drive you?"

"You drive," he said absently as he got up from the sofa and reached for his necktie.

*****

Frank hurried in through the emergency entrance and went to the admissions desk. A kindly, gray-haired nurse was working with papers and she dug deep into the pile in response to Frank's query.

"We didn't find much on him. An identification card with the name William Matson. Nothing else except a wallet initialed W. M. containing thirty-six dollars in cash."

"*Nothing* else?"

The gray-haired nurse shook her head. "No social security number, no driver's license, no home or business address."

"Damned odd, don't you think?"

"Not at Park Hill. We get them in here without a blessed thing but their clothing. In fact, two weeks ago the boys picked up a stark-naked blonde out of a car crash on East River Drive."

Frank grinned automatically, but the grin fell from his face like a mask the moment he turned from the desk. He went through the locker room and got his stethoscope on the way to Ward Five.

The patient known to the hospital as William Matson lay quietly on his back, staring at the ceiling. Frank checked the clipboard. There were no notations but his own. He went around the bed and stood looking down at the patient.

"Feeling better?"

"I feel all—right."

There's some sort of a speech block here, Frank thought as he bent over and lowered the sheet. "I'm just doing a little checking," he said casually. "No cause for alarm."

"I am not—alarmed."

Corson frowned slightly as he concentrated on his work. He went over the patient's torso, up and down, back and forth. At times he straightened to rest his back and stared down into the calm, expressionless face on the pillow.

Twenty minutes passed, during which time Frank Corson checked and rechecked every inch of the man's torso. When he finished, he slowly folded his stethoscope and pulled the sheet back into place. He stared at the patient for a full minute without bringing the slightest change in the empty expression.

"Sleep well," he said, and walked slowly away.

Back in the street, five minutes later, he dropped into the seat beside Rhoda. She eyed him questioningly and when he did not respond, she asked, "Everything all right?"

"I don't know. I guess so."

"What do you mean—guess so? It is or it isn't."

"There was something about a patient's heartbeat. I passed it over on the first examination, but it stuck in my mind. That's why I had to go back."

"And . . . ?"

"He's got two hearts."

"He's *what?*"

"He's got two hearts, my beautiful love. One in his chest, where it ought to be, and one in the center of his lower abdomen."

"You're—you're kidding."

"No, darling," Frank Corson said dreamily. "On this night of nights I found a man who is pretty rare indeed. A man with two healthy, functioning hearts."

"All right," Rhoda asked wonderingly. "What do we do about it?"

"We go home for the time being, baby—to your nice, private, wonderful apartment."

"And . . . ?"

"We make love," he said absently.

*****

Les King, the free-lance news photographer, surveyed his night's work and was not happy. It had been singularly unproductive. A couple of sneak necking shots he'd snapped during a stroll through Central Park had come through a little too pornographic to be of value. Les threw them into the wastebasket. A shot of a man leaning out of a thirtieth-floor window came to nothing because the man had pulled his head in and closed the window. He hadn't jumped. There was a picture of a girl dodging a taxi. He'd caught her with both feet off the ground and a look of surprise on her face, but with her body arced backward and both hands on her rump as though she'd just been thoroughly and expertly goosed. Too vulgar. He put the pic aside.

And the Park Avenue hit? Here it was, a shot of a guy lying where he'd dropped, with the pigeon's rocketing away. Not bad, but it lacked an angle. All that intern had found on him was a name. William Matson. No address. The hell with it.

Les sighed and dropped the pic into his file case. Then he stopped. His face went blank. He pulled the pic out and looked at it again. He felt as if some nagging thought were trying to come to the surface, but nothing clicked, so he dropped the pic back into the file and went to the cooler where he opened an early-morning can of beer before sacking out. A hell of a life, he thought, wandering through nighttime Manhattan watching for people to take their mental pants down so he could get shots of their naked inner backsides.

He finished the beer and went in to take a shower.

Funny about that hit case. The guy had the damnedest expression on his face. Kind of like he was thinking, *Okay, so what do I do now?*

Fifteen minutes later, Les was asleep.

*****

There was always a certain tension involved in Frank Corson's visits to Rhoda Kane's apartment, with Rhoda usually slightly on edge, waiting for one of Frank's outbursts.

An outburst consisted of his suddenly springing to his feet with a scowl and announcing: "Goddamn it, I don't belong here!"

Rhoda always followed the same script at the beginning of these traumas by inevitably asking, "Why, darling? Why must you say that?"

"Oh, hell, Rhoda! I don't want to hurt you but—"

"Darling, you know I'll go to your room with you if you'd be more comfortable there."

He strode to the window angrily and, for Rhoda, there was that indescribably sweet and exciting reaction she always got from his nakedness. *Like a Greek god standing there, she thought*, and it thrilled her even though she knew she was being a little subjective about it.

She smiled with tender, understanding amusement as she realized Frank's pattern never varied. His outbursts never came until the first fierce need of her had been assuaged; this was to her liking because her need was as great.

Reacting according to current, "broad-minded" thinking and Manhattan sophistication, she regarded herself and Frank as having a "good physical relationship." Which individual need was the greatest, she had never been able to say. But there certainly was something extraordinary about it. In analyzing it, she'd arrived at the conclusion that they'd been able, on the basis of personal rapport, to function in a completely uninhibited manner; thus, some of their love-making, when lifted out of context and surveyed objectively, might have been called abnormal. Rhoda did not think so, however; or, if she did, she blocked the idea successfully by telling herself that whatever she and Frank did together was all right because *they* did it. She told herself it was good for them because they looked at it with a healthy attitude.

She could, of course, have gotten this opinion, or one in complete opposition to it, from two different psychologists, but she preferred to play it as she saw it.

She had wondered at times just how important the sex relation was in her attachment to Frank. It was of major importance, of that she was sure, but was it the key? If they drifted apart physically, would the other aspects of the relationship vanish? She thought not, but she certainly would not have been willing to put it to the test.

Frank Corson was through looking out the window now and

he began pacing nervously. "Sure—so it's fine to be a doctor. It's the sure-fire answer for later in life. But what about now? What about this crawling up the ladder inch by inch?" He turned on her defiantly.

"Living on your money!"

"You aren't!"

"All right. Maybe not technically." He looked around the room resentfully. "Using your apartment for—"

"Frank! When I have guests, do they hesitate because my apartment is nicer than—?"

She knew she'd hurt him even before his head came around and his eyes narrowed. "So that's what it really is to you!"

She'd said the wrong thing, but even as she sprang up from the bed she felt that it made no difference because he would have found something else. "I didn't mean it that way. You know I didn't."

She ran to him and laid her hands on his chest; his eyes traveled down her naked body and his mind struggled. His expression said it was a little unfair of her to come so close and stand that way, nude and beautiful and eager, in front of him, especially when he had a point to make.

"I'm a pauper trying to keep up with the rich."

She knew how to break his mood now. She smiled and pressed against him lightly and said, "Uh-huh, but what a pauper. And darling, money wouldn't change that part of it a bit."

He drew her to him violently. The impact of their bodies hurt her ribs but she gloried in the pain. She let her knees weaken and sank to the thickly carpeted floor, bringing him down with her.

She knew Frank's outburst was over—at least for that day.

Later, on the bed, he opened his eyes sleepily. "What time is it?"

"A little after ten."

"That gives us almost two more hours." He looked out over the East River. "It's beautiful."

"*Isn't* it?"

"If I went right into research—took a job somewhere—I could afford to give this to you."

She thought of saying, *But, darling, I've got it already*, and decided a change of subject would be more judicious and said, "You *were* kidding last night, weren't you?"

"Kidding?"

"About the man with two hearts."

Frank grinned a little sheepishly. He was extremely handsome and totally unconscious of it, and when he grinned that way it made him look like a little boy caught stealing jam, and Rhoda always wanted to hug him. But she forebore as he said, "It does seem a little silly, doesn't it?"

"You'd know more about that than I do. Is it silly?"

"Let's say the chances of such a thing happening are rather remote."

"You only used your stethoscope last night?"

"That was all. I went by what I heard."

"What will you do now? X-ray?"

"I'm not sure I'll do anything. The idea is so preposterous."

She regarded him thoughtfully. "It's not like you to lose interest in anything until you know the answer."

He snubbed out his cigarette. "Let's forget Park Hill and funny anatomies, baby. Let's sit on the terrace and bathe ourselves in luxury the way the TV ad says."

And that was the way things stayed for two hours. The time passed swiftly, and when Frank was finally dressed and ready for the street, he refused Rhoda's offer to drive him to the hospital because she was very late, too. He kissed her good-bye, went down the twelve floors in the elevator, and hurried out of the building.

There was no cab in sight and he began to walk. Half a block later he turned a corner and stopped dead. He was facing a man who was coming in the other direction. He stared. The man stared back. Frank automatically stepped aside, but the man did exactly the same thing, at the same time, and they did a little dance there on the sidewalk. Then the man veered around him and moved on up the street. Frank turned and stared after him, then walked slowly in his own direction.

It was the same man. It was the Park Avenue hit. It was the man he'd left in Ward Five with a broken leg. It wasn't a brother or a cousin or a chance resemblance. It was the man himself or an exact double. And what were the percentages against attending a patient one night and meeting his exact double on the street the next morning?

They were fantastic. Like hitting the Irish sweeps.

It was the man. It had to be.

Except that he wasn't broken-legged now. He was walking across the Upper East Side, wearing that same look that was as good as anyone else's, except that you got the impression of an emptiness behind his eyes.

2

Those in the know in Washington, D.C., upon seeing Brent Taber rush to a taxi or dodge a pedestrian on Pennsylvania Avenue, could well say, "There walks power." But there were few indeed who possessed enough knowledge of the Washington inner structure to be able to make this observation.

Brent looked more like a coal heaver than a public servant with a well-oiled escalator into the White House. He appeared more able to direct a gang of dock workers than to jockey a delicate issue through the bloody jungle of national politics. Many of the people who accepted this deception did so at their peril and were not around any more. To others not so foolish, Brent Taber symbolized a completely necessary facet of a working democracy—secret government. This necessity sprang from the realization that even an open society must maintain areas of privacy or it is doomed.

Such was the man, and such was his mission of the moment—an issue of the utmost secrecy. So hush-hush, in fact, was this mission that when Brent Taber arrived at his office that morning and found Senator Crane pacing his reception-room carpet, his heavy eyebrows gathered and he began mentally checking his "tight ship" for a leak.

Senator Crane was the exact opposite of Brent, in that he looked to be exactly what he was; a figure rigidly type-cast to the role of a blustering, tactless servant of the people. Which, in Crane's case, meant that he was a servant of Crane's career and any faction of his supporters that could further it. Still, the Senator could not be called dishonest. He was merely a flexible rationalizer. He sincerely believed that what was good for Crane was good for the "folks back home."

And just now, he felt that a knowledge of what the hell was going on in Brent Taber's orbit was probably not good for anybody and had better be aired.

As Brent entered, Crane came right to the point. "Goddamn it, Taber, just what in blazes is going on around here?"

Brent's thick lips hardly moved, a characteristic that Crane found infuriating because that was the way shady characters talked into Senatorial investigation microphones and it looked pretty bad. But Brent's words came quite clear: "Routine business, Senator—an honest effort to get a day's work done."

"You mean to tell me the meeting that's been set up here is routine?"

Brent shrugged. "Meetings are meetings, Senator."

Crane ticked it off on his fat fingers. "Pender of the Army, Bright of the Navy, Jones of the Air Force, Hagen of the FBI, Wilson from Treasury—they all trooped through here into your private conference room." He pointed pompously at his own chest. "But Crane of the Senate—"

"You forgot Birch of the State Department," Brent cut in. "Or hasn't he arrived yet?"

"—Crane of the Senate is barred! Now just what in the hell—?"

There are times for tact and times for bluntness, and this was a time, Brent decided, for the latter. "What goes on here, Senator," he said, "is none of your business. Otherwise, you would have been invited."

Crane's face darkened and Brent thought pleasantly of a brain hemorrhage blowing the top of his fat head off. But this was too much to hope for.

"Brent," Crane exploded, "I'll get you! So help me, I'll get you! Just who the hell do you think you are—demeaning the dignity of the United States Senate? Just who are you to say what the people should or should not know?"

"Decisions of that nature are made upstairs, Senator. I don't presume to possess the judgment needed in such matters."

"You're an arrogant bureaucrat! Your kind comes and goes because when you get too goddamned arrogant the people rise up in their wrath and knock you off."

Marcia Holly, Brent's secretary, was studiously transcribing some notes and Brent turned his scowl on her because, damn it, she was laughing like hell at the whole thing. And, by God, a secretary didn't have the right to laugh at a United States Senator, even with her eyes, no matter how much a congenital idiot he was.

"I'm sorry, Senator," Brent said. "If you have a complaint, please take it up with my superiors. Just now I—"

"Your superiors? And who the devil are they? Who can find them? Where do they have offices? Go around trying to find your superiors and nobody ever heard of you."

Brent half smiled as he felt a sneaking admiration for Crane. The son-of-a-bitch had a disarming quality of honesty. If he planned to knife you, he drove straight in, the knife held high.

"One of the disadvantages of being a negative personality, Senator," Brent murmured.

"Sure! You're about as negative as a charging grizzly," Crane snorted and headed for the door as though his air had been cut off.

After his bulk had vanished into the corridor, Brent turned a scowl on Marcia Holly. "And what are you snickering about."

She raised large blue, innocent eyes. "Me? I? Oh, golly. I just found a cute little Freudian slip in these notes and—"

"Shut up. Are they all here?"

"Birch of the State Department sent regrets. A duty call on the Tasmanian Embassy or something."

"Okay—and next week he'll be screaming to high heaven about being left out."

Marcia's laughing eyes agreed. "Ain't it the truth?" she marveled.

Brent strode past her and expertly mussed her sleek hairdo in a quick gesture. As he entered his private conference room, he turned and grinned at her silent fury.

Inside, they were all waiting for him, seated around a teakwood table. The wall-to-wall carpeting was wine-red. The chairs were deep and upholstered. And the men who sat in them were distinguished only by their surroundings and their uniforms. Their metal and their worth were hidden inside.

Brent moved to the end of the table and scanned them moodily. "Okay, gentlemen. I'll talk. Then if you have any questions— shoot them." He took a deep breath and began:

"We are faced with a situation that must be kept top secret for two reasons: First, it may be the first move in an attempt to subjugate or destroy our planet; two, it is so utterly ridiculous on its face that a public announcement would be greeted by hoots of laughter from pole to pole." Brent's ugly scowl deepened at what he seemed to feel was an injustice. "Even the Eskimos would get a yack out of it."

The group waited, withholding judgment, evidently waiting to see whether or not it was a laughing matter. They were conceding nothing. Brent studied them for a moment and then went on.

"Last week, in Denver, early in the morning," he said, "a man was found dead on a residential-section street. There was no apparent cause of death. A routine autopsy revealed some peculiar things about the man's insides. For one thing, he had two hearts—"

Jones of the Air Force, a dignified, gray-haired man, paused in firing his cigar and gave the impression he was lighting his way through the darkness. Bright of the Navy, a thin man with a huge Adam's apple, allowed it to bob three times in deference to the startling nature of Brent's statement. Pender of the Army raised one eyebrow and let it fall. To a keen observer, Hagen of the FBI would have revealed prior knowledge by reacting not at all.

His mind was on the kid. He was thinking, Christ! With all the damned miracle drugs and characters orbiting the earth in crazy capsules, they still haven't figured out a way to keep a six-year-old from getting a cold. He remembered the kid waving from the window yesterday morning—when he'd been ordered East to attend this clambake—standing there beside Miriam, waving good-bye and barking like a sea lion. What the hell was wrong with doctors? Why didn't they get with it on a stupidly simple thing like the common cold?

". . . two hearts and—" Brent reached to the left and pulled down a chart on a window shade-type rack that stood beside his chair, "—a rather interesting arrangement of the internal organs." He pointed with a thick finger. "You'll notice that the liver is exceptionally small, while the kidneys are large enough to service a horse. You'll note also that while the man had testicles, there is no prostrate gland."

The group waited in a kind of guarded abeyance that could be easily sensed. Their silence gave the impression that they were asking: *Is somebody kidding us?*

But there was certainly no lightness in Brent's manner. His arm dropped and he scowled at the far end of the table as he said, "Now, the blood. There was something strange about the blood—"

The door from Marcia Holly's reception room-office opened and she came in silently, followed by a white-coated waiter who set a tray on the table. The coffeepot on the tray was silver; the cups, fine china; the napkins, linen.

"—something very strange about the blood in that it conformed to all necessary specifications and yet it had a synthetic quality about it . . ."

Goose pimples formed on Hagen's neck and walked gently down his spine. Nothing was missing in this setup—synthetic blood, two hearts, oversize kidneys. Hagen got a quick mental flash of a barker outside a circus sideshow: *He walks like a man. He talks like a man. But for a thin dime, folks, you can see—*

It was something to think and wonder about. And back in Chicago, he'd had lots of company. Everybody in the office that night had wondered, and you could see the vague uneasiness in their eyes as the creature sat, acting like a human being and, at the same time, like nothing from this world. You could see a vague revulsion in the people surrounding the creature. There was also uncertainty, and this from men who were required by their profession to be fairly certain about most things.

"The blood," Jones of the Air Force said. "Could it have been a—well, a new kind of plasma?"

"Hardly. You see, the variation was almost theoretical, if you can understand the term as I'm using it. Drawn from an ordinary human being, it would not have been questioned. It was just that in the light of other oddities in his man, it didn't seem right, somehow."

"Pretty vague," Bright of the Army said.

"This I'll grant you." Brent said. "Anybody for coffee?"

Nobody was for coffee so Marcia and the waiter retired and Brent said, "Vague, I'll grant you. But let's get on with it. Two days later, a man, in every way identical, was found lying in the street in Pittsburgh, Pennsylvania. He was alive, but in a dying condition, and he succumbed on the way to the hospital. Cause of death, as in the first place, undeterminable. But the medics think it was some malfunctioning of the lungs.

"All in all, gentlemen, eight identical specimens have been picked up in various American cities. Five are dead, two more are now in a comatose condition, at last report, and may very well be dead at this time. One is still alive and relatively healthy. . . ."

Alive and relatively healthy. The son-of-a-bitch! Hagen felt an odd senseless rage against the creature they'd picked up in a Chicago bar.

Ordinarily it would have been a simple bull-pen, night-court case—a loud-mouth drunk refusing to pay for a drink. But much of his talk, anent enemy invasion, internal destruction, and civilian chaos, had been a little too rough for the other barflies to swallow, and complaints had been made. Later, when Bureau men went around trying to get something tangible in the way of evidence, they found themselves dealing in frustration. The complainants had left without giving their names. The barkeep really hadn't heard anything. The actual charges had gone up in smoke. But by that time, Washington was very much interested. The man was questioned and it was the damnedest thing Hagen had ever gone through . . .

"By identical," Jones of the Air Force said, "you of course mean—"

Brent's dark, knifelike eyes sliced out at Jones. "By identical, I mean just that."

Bright's throat bobbed as the astonishing implication came home to him. "Hell, man! You mean—"

"I mean these specimens do not merely bear a resemblance to each other. They were not just similar as to organisms and physical structure. They were all *exactly* alike; as alike as eight new cars of the same make and model lined up side by side . . ."

Identical. Hagen didn't know anything about that. He hadn't seen the others. But he knew that there was something frightening about the one they'd picked up in Chicago. At first glance he could have been Mr. Anybody, from Anywhere, U.S.A. A youngish-looking forty, you would have figured, with a sprinkling of gray at the temples and a face women could have found interesting. He had the unpaunched figure of a man who had taken good care of himself; he was quietly dressed in a blue suit; he looked like a decent-enough guy who just happened to have gotten stiff on the double hooker he'd ordered and sounded off without meaning to.

In fact, he was still sounding off when they got him into the interrogation room. And when the barflies called his talk treasonable, they hadn't been fooling.

Brent said, "Identical, gentlemen, even to the finger-prints; to the very last ridge."

Pender's eyebrows tried to crawl up his forehead and disappear into his hairline. "That's utterly and completely ridiculous."

Brent smiled. "Then, at least, I've gotten one idea over to you—that a public release on this thing would be greeted with hoots of derision by the realistic American public."

"And perhaps deservedly so?"

"I think not," Brent said gravely.

Is it some incredibly ingenious hoax? Hagen asked himself the question and found no answer. He only remembered the words and the eyes and the tone of the creature that walked like a man . . .

"He was our—father. They had him a long time before we—

came. He was our father, and after we came they told us what we were to know and we knew—it."

There it was—that odd little break, cutting off the word at the end of each sentence. It gave the impression of a mind groping, yet not really groping; a mind sure of itself, yet wondering.

"What did you know?"

"We knew what we were—for. Our—reason. We knew what we were created to do—here."

"How many of you were there?"

"Ten of—us."

"You said, 'created to do here.' Where do you come from?"

"There."

"Where is *there*?"

At this point the man or the creature, or whatever you wanted to call him, pointed upward.

At this point, Cantrell, another of the interrogation group, turned away in disgust. "A kook! A kook with a religious compulsion. A character, and we got called out of bed to—"

"—to get you ready to be destroyed," the creature cut in.

"By fire and brimstone on judgment day?" Cantrell asked sarcastically.

"No. By rendering you helpless by—"

Here the creature swallowed, blinked and looked surprised—and changed magically. He—if it really was a he—didn't jump up and kick a hole in the ceiling or anything like that. In fact, nothing tangible happened. There just seemed to be an invisible barrier that rose suddenly around him.

Then there was the thing that chilled every man in the room; a thing as tangible as the walls and the furniture; yet a thing no man could define in words.

This was when Cantrell, a high-strung individual at best, reacted violently to the change in the creature. In an instinctive blaze of anger and frustration, Cantrell reached out and slapped him brutally across the face.

Velie, the agent in charge, also acted instinctively as he lunged forward to restrain Cantrell. But then he froze, as did all the men in the room, to stare.

It was not what the prisoner did; it was what he did not do. There was absolutely no reaction to the blow—no reaction physically, emotionally, or mentally. It was as though the blow had not been struck; as though this were some kind of a moving, breathing zombie.

So tangible, so seemingly sourceless was this feeling of loathing, that Hagen would have been sure it had affected only himself if he had not seen its effect on the others.

Yet none of them referred to it. Nor was this strange, because there just weren't any words to describe the feeling one gets from contact with a pleasant-faced, quietly dressed example of the walking dead.

Backing away from this powerful emotional reaction, Hagen forced himself onto an intellectual level, and asked himself what had brought about the change in the creature. Why had it—Hagen now had to regard the strange, walking enigma as neuter—after functioning to some extent as a human, reverted suddenly to what seemed to be its natural state?

He conceded that if he knew the answer to that one, he could be of great service to the FBI and the nation—and, no doubt to the world . . .

Pender of the Army now had a question. "What information have you gotten from the surviving man?"

"Not a great deal, as yet. However, in our experiments we've learned something rather frightening."

"And what's that?"

"He is totally impervious to drugs of any description whatever."

"That's impossible!"

"So it would seem. But the sodium pentathol injection he was given could just as well have been so much water."

The group pondered this information, each after his own fashion. Then Birch of the State Department made a precise, scholarly observation. "Incredible!"

Brent smiled faintly. "One point of vital importance. We do know that there were, originally, ten of these creatures roaming the country. Eight are accounted for. The other two are still at large."

Jones of the Air Force asked, "Were all eight apprehended in large cities?"

"Yes."

"Shouldn't that mean something to us?"

"Well, it's a pattern, all right, but no one's been able to give it any meaning—so far."

No one had any further comment on that point. Brent waited

a moment and then threw the bombshell. "We are quite sure that these creatures are of extraterrestrial origin."

For a time it seemed as though Brent's bombshell had been a dud. There was no comment from around the table—no sound of any kind. But each man was evaluating the information after his own fashion. The key thought, no doubt, other than a natural and instinctive moment of sheer unbelief, was that this marked a giant, forward lunge in world history. And also, no doubt, in this group of responsible men, there was a common question: It would appear that our world had at last come to grips with the universe around it. Was our world ready?

And there was general doubt.

Now the questions came. From whence? To what purpose? Hostile? Benign? Dangerous? Harmless?

"What other information was gained from the creature?"

"Very little. He knows our language. He is here for a definite and clear-cut purpose. Probably hostile. But what he was supposed to do or how he was supposed to accomplish it we do not know."

"Do you think you will eventually get these answers?"

"I think," and there was an ominous note in Brent's voice, "that we will. If not from the creature himself, then in some sudden and far more violent manner."

This statement also had impact. It seemed that the group had overlooked Brent's previous revelation that ten of the creatures had arrived and only eight had been accounted for.

"Perhaps," Jones said hopefully, "whatever their plan, it required the participation of all ten."

"In that case," Brent said quietly, "we have nothing to worry about. At least, at the moment."

"Are you of the opinion that these creatures have been dropped anywhere else on earth?"

"All I can say on that score is that all seems quiet around the world. Of course, if Russia has rounded up a quota of these two-hearted characters they wouldn't be likely to tell us. They certainly haven't shown up in the European countries with whom we consult. All I can say about the situation behind the Iron Curtain is that they have made no inquiries of us relative to the matter—and we certainly have made no inquiries of them. Also, our people in the sensitive Eastern areas report nothing indicative."

Pender bobbed his throat and said, "You told us you're sure

the creatures are from outer space. That makes our interests with Russia mutual. Therefore, why shouldn't open inquiry be made?"

Brent frowned. "An entirely logical question. As a matter of fact, I recommended that course. Nothing has been down in that direction, however. At least, not to my knowledge."

"I assume the White House knows about this."

Brent nodded but did not elaborate, perhaps because to have done so would have tended to clarify his own connection with the top spot in the nation; a relationship accepted but not thoroughly understood by any man present.

"May I inquire as to Senator Crane?" Bright asked.

"I see no reason why you shouldn't."

"He was in your anteroom when I entered. Obviously he was mad. I assume that was because you excluded him from this meeting."

"Correct." Brent Taber's eyes turned a trifle steely. "In fact, I'd like to know exactly how he found out about the meeting."

No one offered any data on this point and Bright asked, "Is it wise to keep information of this vital nature from the United States Senate?"

"The information has not been kept from the United States Senate," Brent corrected. "Let's say it has been kept from certain United States Senators on the theory that the interests of the nation can best be served by a closed-door policy on this matter until it becomes clarified."

Whether they agreed or not, the men present accepted this as coming from the top, and they would automatically abide by it.

"I suppose," Pender said, "that every effort is being made to apprehend the missing pair."

"Every effort of which we are capable."

"What conclusions have you drawn from the fact that these ten creatures are identical?"

"That they are not human beings, in the strictest sense of the word," Brent replied gravely.

"Then what are they?"

"We believe they are androids."

"And what the hell is an android?" Jones snapped.

"A synthetic." Brent smiled just slightly. "In this case, men not born of women. All this is detailed in the confidential report that will be handed to you when you leave. The report, incidentally, is slanted in a way that obscures its vital nature, but on the basis of what has been said at this meeting, I'm sure you'll find all your answers."

Brent paused, waiting for questions. When none came, he said, "I guess that about covers it, gentlemen—at least, all that we have at the moment. You'll be kept informed. The meeting is adjourned."

He glanced around. "Oh, by the way, as you'll note in the confidential report, this project will be identified as 'Operation Blue Sky.'"

"Where did they get that one?" Jones snorted.

"I don't know. The term originated higher up. Possibly," Brent murmured, "because somewhere out in the blue sky lies the answer." His manner changed and he glanced briskly around. "Would anyone care for a cup of coffee?"

No one was interested in coffee and the group filed out.

*****

Ten minutes later, the white-coated waiter came to pick up the things. He crossed to the coffeepot, lifted it, and took a tiny device out of the hidden space formed by the pot's legs and its bottom. This, he slipped into his pocket before picking up the tray and going out as he'd come.

3

Frank Corson got what was possibly the greatest shock of his life when he walked into Ward Five and saw William Matson lying in bed. It wasn't so much that he hadn't expected it. He had, because he was too firmly locked in reality to believe the man he saw on the Upper East Side could possibly have been the broken-legged Matson. Still, seeing Matson in bed had the effect of bringing unreality into a realm where he had to cope with it. Perhaps, during the trip back to the hospital, he'd been mystically apprised of what lay ahead and wanted subconsciously to avoid it. Perhaps his shock was a cringing away from facing a problem.

At the moment, of course, he didn't know what the problem was. There was a mystery here, but only that, and his first thought was to report it to higher authority—the business about the two hearts—and have it investigated. With this thought in mind, he walked down the corridor and reached for the knob of the door marked *Superintendent*.

But quite suddenly he stopped, reversed himself, and went back to Ward Five. He approached Matson's bed and looked down at him. Matson, empty of expression, stared back, and again Frank Corson sensed rather than saw the emptiness behind the eyes.

"How are you feeling?"

"I feel very—well."

"It wasn't a bad break. How would you like to leave the hospital?"

"I would like to leave the—hospital."

Frank felt an odd, inner frustration. What in the devil was wrong with the man? He sounded like a child just learning the language. Yet there was nothing else to indicate backwardness. He looked pretty much like a self-sufficient, self-contained adult.

"I can sign you out—get you a pair of crutches. By the way, I don't think the hospital got your home address."

"My home—address?"

"Yes. The place you live." There was a pause, and finally Frank realized the man wasn't going to answer. "Your home, man. Where you live."

"I'm looking for a—home."

"Oh, I see. New in town?"

"Yes, new in—town."

"I have a place," Frank said, and it seemed to him as though someone else were talking from within him—that he was only a listener. "You can crowd in with me until you get settled somewhere."

"I can crowd in with—you?"

"Okay?"

"Okay."

"Fine, I'll see that you're signed out. Ever walk on crutches before?"

"I never walked on—crutches."

"Nothing much to it. You'll get the knack."

Frank left the bed and headed toward the office, asking himself as he went, *Why in hell did I do that?* Then he found the reason—or at least a reason that would suffice.

The discovery of a man with two hearts might be worth something. At least, it would put Frank Corson, unknown intern, into the spotlight for a while. This was pretty vague thinking but it made a kind of sense and Frank settled for it in lieu of trying to analyze the strange compulsion, the odd foreboding deep within him.

Here's a thing that might do me some good, he told himself. Why not take advantage of it?

Perhaps he was rigidly blocking out the cause of his unrest—that he was more or less dependent upon Rhoda Kane for the luxuries that were involved in seeing her, having a relationship with her. He could neither ask her to dine with him on his level, at some place like Nedick's, nor could he refuse to go with her to The Forum or the Four Seasons. He could not take her to his miserable furnished room on East 13th Street, nor refuse rendezvous in her Upper East Side apartment.

He was trapped and was thus desperately looking for a way out.

And somehow, grotesquely, there were indications that a man with two hearts might help to provide the answer.

*****

The tape recorder stuck to the bottom of the Taber conference coffeepot had cost Senator Crane a hundred dollars. He had now listened to it four times and was pacing the floor of his office, scowling darkly at the walls. An android! What in hell was an android? What kind of a stupid, impossible thing was this?

In a flash of panic, Crane wondered if it was all a diabolical machination of Brent Taber's. Maybe Taber knew all about the recorder. Maybe the whole meeting was an elaborate plant to maneuver an earnest, alert senator into making a public fool of himself. Taber was certainly capable of such a thing.

And that was how it had begun to look. Still, that was ridiculous. The Army, the Navy, the Air Force—they were all involved. Only Congress—the true representatives of the people—had been ignored. And, by God, he'd do something about it!

Crane stopped pacing but continued to scowl at the wall. Now, what department of research could find him some data on androids?

*****

Les King was awakened by a knock on his door. He rolled over, blinked and looked at his watch. A little after two in the afternoon, which was equivalent to midnight for Les. He pulled on his robe and went to the door and opened it.

He blinked.

Sure, no doubt about it. The man standing there was the one he'd snapped on Park Avenue the other A.M., lying among a bunch of pigeons, with a broken leg. But evidently that hadn't been the case because his legs were okay now. It couldn't even have been a sprain, judging by the way he was standing there. He was a fairly tall, good-looking guy in his middle forties maybe—brown hair, blue eyes with a kind of vacant look about them.

And there was something else, goddamn it; something that kept evading Les; something that had bothered him when he'd first developed the print. *Let's see, what is this guy's name? The ambulance intern found it in his jacket pocket on a half-torn identification card. William Matson.*

But, damn it, there was something else.

"Mr. Lester—King?"

"Right. What can I do for you?"

"I had trouble in locating—you. I wish to make a—purchase."

Queer duck. Damned queer. "What can I sell you?"

"You are a—photographer. You took a picture of a man injured on Park—Avenue. I wish to buy that—picture."

Les knotted his robe and stepped back. "Sure. Come on in."

The man entered the room and stood silent while Les got out his file. "What do you want it for?" he asked.

"It is for my personal—use."

"Sure." Les handed the glossy to the man he identified in his own mind as Matson. "That the one?"

After a grave inspection, the other replied, "Yes. How much does it cost—me?"

"Ten bucks?"

Without comment, the man sorted a ten-dollar bill from a skimpy roll he took from his pocket and handed it to Les. With that, he turned and walked out, closing the door after him and leaving several questions in Les King's mind. Was this a vanity operation? Had the guy merely wanted a glossy of himself? He hadn't impressed Les as being that kind of man. Was there a reason for wanting the pic off the market? That didn't make sense either because he hadn't asked for the negative.

Quite suddenly, in answer to the really important, the nagging, question, Les snapped his fingers. The hem of his dressing gown flapped around his skinny legs as he dived to his old file rack and went back where the dust was thick. He brought out an envelope, dug into it, and found what he was looking for—an old newspaper clipping dated some ten years back. It consisted of a headline:

LOCAL POLITICIAN DISAPPEARS

The clipping was from the Kenton, New York, *Chronicle*, an upstate weekly, and the news story told how Judge Sam Baker had vanished on a fishing trip to a nearby lake. Accidental drowning had been the verdict but, as yet, the body had not been recovered.

Les King stared at the clipping. The body, as he remembered it, never was recovered, either, but the drowning verdict stood intact and the judge had been gradually forgotten.

Les King's interest in the affair had been financial. He'd gone to Kenton, talked Baker's widow out of a couple of family photographs, and had hiked back to New York, hoping for a sale to a big daily.

But the story hadn't caught on even though it well might have, because Baker's power extended into Albany and could thus have interested New York City. All in all, it had been a profitless speculation on Les King's part.

Now, however, it seemed to be coming to life again. Les stared at the photo under the headline. It was a good one—exceptionally clear.

And beyond a shadow of a doubt, it was the man who had just

come to Les King's room to purchase a glossy of himself for ten dollars. No wonder the sight of that stranger had nagged at Les. He'd seen that face before.

"Now just what in the hell have we got here?" Les mused. Something definitely worth looking into, that was for sure.

He reached for his pants.

4

Dr. Rudolph Entman, one of the world's foremost neurologists, stripped off his rubber gloves and scowled at the strange body that lay on the table before him.

"Goddamn it," he fumed, "it's artificially constructed. It's been hand-made—manufactured. And there's one thing I'd give a few years of my life to know."

Brent Taber stared moodily into Entman's myopic little eyes and asked, "What's that, Doctor?"

"How in hell did they do it?"

"Who do you suppose *they* are?"

Entman looked ceilingward in a manner that indicated he might either be hunting for *them* somewhere out beyond, or sending a prayer heavenward in a plea for Divine counsel and guidance.

"Some form of entity with far greater intelligence than we possess."

"You can tell me more than that, can't you?" Brent asked sharply. And when Doctor Entman looked up in surprise, he added, "Sorry for the tone. My nerves have gotten a little edgy lately."

Entman smiled understandingly. "I don't wonder. As to this living machine—no . . . it's not a machine because it did *live*. Let's see what we can figure out. What's it made of? The material used in its construction is—oh, hell—how can I put it? This way, maybe. Take a wool blanket and call it genuine flesh, blood and bone. Now, take a blanket made of one of the new synthetics—Dacron or any one of the other equally serviceable materials—call that the material this creature is made of. Figuring it that way—"

"You mean our visitor's body is constructed of things that feel and look like flesh, blood and bone—work as well, but aren't. Right?"

"Right. But, of course, that doesn't tell you anything you didn't know before."

"But what about their potentials, their capabilities? They're *human*—in the sense that they're exact duplicates of humans—and they *live*, but what about emotions? If we accept the somewhat unscientific theory that it's a soul which is responsible for feelings and emotions, these . . . these . . . creatures would be handicapped." Brent paused as if uncertain of his ground.

"Wouldn't they?" he asked lamely. "I mean, they couldn't—theoretically, at least—react to situations . . . or other people's emotions."

Doctor Entman nodded his head and murmured, "I would be inclined to agree. Except that we're obviously dealing with superior intelligence—I'm speaking about the 'people' responsible for these androids—and we have no idea how far they might have progressed in duplicating that indefinable something we call a soul."

For a moment he lapsed into silence. Then looked up at Brent abruptly. "Have you read anything on Kendrick's experiments with synthetic emotion?"

"Can't say that I have."

"Kendrick, down at Penton Technological Institute, has done some remarkable things in drawing the stuff of human emotion from one person, holding it on a tape, and transferring it to another person."

"On the face of it, that sounds ridiculous."

"Doesn't it? Nevertheless, the vibrations set up, or created you might say, by a person in anger, consist of some sort of *stuff*—in the sense of an incredibly high frequency wave. Radio or television waves are the best comparisons.

"Kendrick, in one demonstration, took a young man who was very much in love with a certain young lady. A really love-sick lad. He placed him in the recording unit gave him the young lady's picture, and told him to let his mind dwell on her to the exclusion of all else."

Doctor Entman smiled briefly. "This, I imagine, wasn't difficult for the lad to do. Entman then put another young man, one who was unacquainted with the girl, into a receiving unit and exposed him, after giving him the girl's picture, to the vibrations created by the lovelorn chap. Later, they saw to it that the second lad was introduced to the girl. The results were rather startling, in that the young lady suddenly had two ardent suitors in place of one."

Brent Taber scratched his ear and looked dubious. "That sounds pretty sensational. But maybe the second lad just plain happened to fall in love with the girl by natural processes."

"True, but the experiments tended to eliminate that possibility. Other emotions were tested. How about a man walking up to a man he'd never seen before in his life and busting him in the nose?"

"Okay, okay. Then you think—"

"I think a lot of things. Here, I see the possibility of a race with superior science, having moved far ahead of us in the directions Kendrick is pointing toward in his research. For instance, with more advanced knowledge and know-how, they've probably been able to charge a synthetic body with a complete set of functioning emotional responses. Grant them that and we can also concede a tailor-made ego."

"I don't mind admitting I'm scared, Doctor," Brent Taber said.

"I think it's a time to be scared."

"But if a race of people were that advanced, if their intention is hostile, why do they pussyfoot around this way? Why don't they just come down and take us over?"

"I've wondered that, too. And yet, a race on some planet out there in the universe might not evolve according to what we consider a logical pattern."

"What do you mean?"

"I mean that while they can create a synthetic man, their interests, and therefore their progress, may have stayed in peaceful channels. For instance, they may not have bothered with anything as elementary as the atom bomb."

"It's a thought."

"A wishful thought, I'll admit. But it does have some validity. Also, it has a fact of some possible value to back it up."

"What fact?"

"That they *haven't* come down and taken us over."

"You almost cheer me, Doctor. Almost, but not quite."

"Actually," Entman said, "I've been wondering about something else."

"What's that?"

"When and how they came here before."

"You mean, where did they get the model for the ten androids?"

"Yes. They had to have not only a model, but also some knowledge concerning our geographical and atmospheric conditions. The two hearts indicate that they knew the elements contained in our air—the pressures and so forth necessary to our existence—and were unable to construct a working model that would function under our conditions with a single heart. So they put in two."

"It looks as though they missed on some other things, too. Seven of the androids have expired."

Entman shrugged. "Still—a remarkable job, particularly since they would have no chance for a trial-and-error test under the conditions that would prevail. It's surprising that *any* of the androids were able to keep functioning."

"The eighth one is pretty sick. He may be gone by now. And about their earlier coming, I can give you one point. They came quietly, probably at night, grabbed their model, and moved out fast."

"How do you know that?"

"Because, obviously, they think all men on earth look alike. Or, at least, we can assume that. Else how did they expect to get away with ten identical androids?"

Entman's eyes widened. "I never thought of that," he muttered.

*****

Senator Crane, a doggedly determined man, had listened to the replay of Brent Taber's top-secret conference again and again. In the comfortable rationalization of which he was capable, his whole zeal and hostility were fashioned around Brent's "arrogant disregard of democratic processes." Who did this bureaucrat think he was? Did he consider himself smarter than the People? Did he feel they couldn't be trusted with revelations affecting their survival? Well, by God, they'd been trusted with word of the bomb and its implications, and they'd reacted admirably. So they were entitled to frankness concerning this new threat to their security.

Of course, Senator Crane reserved the right to enlighten them in his own time and in his own way. After all, hadn't they elected him and thus given him leeway to use his own judgment in their best interests?

But who the hell had elected Brent Taber?

Nobody.

So Crane listened to the recording and picked out what he classified as the key lines.

A routine autopsy revealed some peculiar things . . . The man had two hearts. . . .

The blood? Could it have been a new kind of plasma? . . .

All in all, gentlemen, eight identical specimens have been picked up in various American cities . . .

Exactly alike. . . .

Crane ran through the rest of it and threw himself moodily into a chair. The idiots! The stupid unelected, self-appointed guardians of democracy! Not once—not *once*, mind you—had a single one of these great brains referred to the obvious.

It was a Russian plot!

All those allusions to the extraterrestrial was so much bilge. The Russians were infiltrating the country with synthetic men. This meant—oh, God—it meant that in a short time Russia would be able to create an army of these monsters and overwhelm the world.

Senator Crane sprang to his feet and measured his indignation in long strides across the thick, expensive carpeting on his floor. The traitor! The sheer, compulsive opportunist! That was certainly all that Brent Taber could be called. Using this deadly situation as a means of furthering his own interests.

Senator Crane deliberately stilled his rage and objectively considered what he should do about it. With the obvious source of the androids logically deduced, there was only his own defensive procedures to be considered. And they had to be considered carefully. As he saw himself, he stood alone, against a group of bumbling idiots, with the future of the nation at stake. What to do?

The key question, of course, was: How soon will Russia be able to mount an army? Probably not very soon, he decided. That fact gave him time to ferret out more information; to become completely sure of himself.

One thing you had to realize about the American public—or about any mass of humanity, for that matter—a thing of importance had to be presented dramatically. This, in a sense, was the duty of the elected public servant—to recognize this somewhat childish failing of the average intelligence and make allowances for it. *You can do this, of course*, Senator Crane told himself, *when you love the people.*

And, fortunately for their survival, Senator Crane loved the American people.

So, for a few moments, he o'erleaped the hard work ahead and saw the goal—envisioned the headlines:

SENATOR CRANE UNCOVERS
DEADLY PERIL TO THE NATION

Due entirely to the patriotic, selfless efforts of one United States Senator, the nation has been warned in time of. . . .

SENATOR CRANE STUNS CONGRESS
AND THE NATION WITH HIS REVELATIONS

Standing alone on the rostrum, a heroic figure pitted, as it were, against all the sinister forces that bore from within, one valiant United States Senator. . . .

Crane had dropped back into his chair. His eyes had closed, the better to visualize a grateful nation expending their plaudits.

And because he was a man who used a great deal of energy in pursuing an objective, he tired at times. He became drowsy now. . . .

. . . And went gently to sleep.

5

"Doctor Corson. Calling Doctor Corson. Please come to the second-floor reception room."

Frank Corson got the call as he was leaving the maternity ward. He took the elevator down and found a rather sloppily dressed, middle-aged man sitting on a lounge beside a weather-beaten camera that tended to mark his profession.

"I'm Les King, a free-lance news photographer. You're Doctor Corson?"

Frank Corson's reaction was slightly hostile. He wondered why. "I'm Doctor Corson."

"I'm on the trail of a patient that came here late last night. Name, William Matson. They tell me he was your patient."

Frank nodded briefly.

"They say he was released."

"That's right."

"A little over an hour ago."

"Right."

"They say he had a broken leg."

"If that's what they said, it must be a matter of record."

"Well, they're wrong on both counts. He came to see me over three hours ago—and both his legs were as good as mine."

Frank Corson did not volunteer the information that he had personally taken William Matson to his furnished room in Greenwich Village and that Matson was there at this very moment, awaiting Frank's return.

"I think there must be some mistake on your part," Frank said.

"No mistake. But something very definitely got crossed up. Maybe we ought to have a little talk—the two of us."

Anger stirred in Frank Corson. Did this Les King character think a beaten-up camera gave him the right to walk in and make demands. "I'm busy now. And I can't see what we'd have to talk about."

"A hell of a lot, maybe. There are some things you may not know about this deal. You might have let a big thing slip through your fingers."

"Look here, I'm not interested in anything you've got to say. And I think you've got a hell of a nerve, coming in here and cross-examining me on something that's—"

King reacted with weary patience. "Take it easy. I'm just trying to get some information that can help both of us, maybe."

"How could it possibly help me?"

"To make it simple, there's a standing ten-thousand-dollar reward for knowledge of the whereabouts of a Judge Sam Baker who disappeared ten years ago from a little upstate New York town. Now, if you aren't interested—"

"Are you telling me that William Matson is Sam Baker?"

"Let's say a hell of a lot indicates it. Matson left here without giving a home address. If you know what it is, we can do business. If you don't—"

"I'm off duty in an hour," Frank Corson said. "Maybe we should talk it over."

"That's better. In the meantime, if you'll tell me where I can find Matson—"

Frank smiled. "Wait an hour. Then I'll show you. But we'll talk about it first."

*****

The tenth android, one of the two so earnestly sought after by Brent Taber, had observed the accident at 59th Street and Park Avenue on the previous night. He'd stood on the curb, lost in the crowd that gathered, and had watched the proceedings carefully. A man who was not a man, a machine that was not a machine, he incorporated, in many respects, the best qualities of both. Now, as the leader of the group deposited from space for a specific purpose, he exhibited these qualities excellently.

He waited. He observed. He added the accident to the several other unforeseen incidents that endangered the project and its objective, and stored them in his memory-bank.

He watched the minor drama as it unfolded, and what was somewhat akin to a danger bell went off in his mind when he saw a bright flash, traced its source to a camera, and carefully studied the man who had taken the picture. Pictures, he knew, could be dangerous. He must get his hands on the picture, if possible.

He waited. He observed. He evaluated. The situation had gotten somewhat out of his control, but he did not blame himself for this. Certain emotions had been made a part of his being, but guilt, a useless one, had been omitted, as had been any ability to react to love, compassion, anger or hatred.

So, with no hope of reward or fear of punishment, he had recorded the facts that he had been unable to communicate tele-pathically with eight of the units under his command and that, therefore, they were no longer operational. He had no way of knowing what had happened to them. This, however, did not make his work one bit less vital. Even though eight units were unaccounted for, his intelligent handling of the ninth android, and of himself, was still vitally important. It was up to him to see that the project was brought to a successful conclusion.

He watched as the ambulance came, noted the name of the hospital, and recorded the proceedings. But he allowed the ambulance to drive away, keeping his attention pointed at the man who had taken the picture.

When the man moved off down the street, the tenth android followed. When the man entered Central Park, he was observed from a discreet distance. When he came out again, he was followed into Times Square, down into Greenwich Village, back uptown and, finally, to an apartment building in the West Seventies. There he was observed opening a mailbox, and the name thereon was duly recorded.

At this point, temporarily entrusting King to destiny, the tenth android took a taxicab to the Park Hill Hospital where he entered, went to the desk, and inquired about a friend of his, a William Matson.

He was directed to Emergency where a nurse, after checking a record sheet on her piled-up desk, told him that Doctor Corson was with the patient in Ward Five. Unaware that he had been extremely lucky, that very few real people—people with only one heart, and a soul to go with it—would have gotten such specific information out of a receiving-desk nurse, the tenth android began counting wards until he came to the one marked Five.

He looked in through the small window in the swinging door and saw his counterpart in bed, a white-coated man bending over him.

That made the ninth android unapproachable, so his counterpart-leader withdrew to the end of the corridor and waited until Doctor Corson came out. He followed Corson outside and, from the back seat of another taxi, never lost sight of the convertible until Rhoda Kane drove it into the garage under her apartment building. From the street, the tenth android saw Rhoda and Frank enter the elevator. As soon as the door closed, he was in the outer lobby, watching as the numbers progressed upward on the elevator dial. The hand stopped at 21. This was noted and recorded, after which the tenth android called a finish to the night's activities and retired to the small room he'd rented on a quiet street on the Lower East Side where, if you bothered no one, no one would bother you.

He was back the next morning, however, and that's when his unavoidable contact with Frank Corson on the sidewalk was made. He noted the surprise on Corson's face, but the logical situation did not develop because Corson did not make an issue of the meeting. He allowed the tenth android to go on his way.

A nonsynthetic man would have wondered at this and thanked his own good luck. Not so with the android. He knew nothing whatever about luck. He accepted this bit of good fortune in exactly the same manner he would have faced its opposite, and when Frank Corson boarded a bus, a taxicab pulled out of a side street and followed.

The cab waited, in front of the Park Hill Hospital. When Frank Corson and the ninth android emerged, two cabs, not one, wheeled down Manhattan and into Greenwich Village.

Thus it was that some ten minutes after Frank Corson went back to his duties at the Park Hill Hospital, there was a knock on the door of his room in Greenwich Village. The ninth android opened the door. The tenth android entered. The ninth android hobbled back to his chair and waited quietly.

The tenth android looked both ways in the corridor and then closed the door. He walked to the chair and stood looking down. He turned his eyes to the bulky, cast-encased leg. "It will not heal," he stated matter-of-factly.

The ninth android nodded. "I—know."

"That makes you useless."

Another nod. "Why couldn't they have made it possible for our flesh and bone to become whole again after an—accident?"

"That wasn't possible."

The tenth android went to a tiny curtained-off kitchenette and returned with a knife. He put his hand on the head of the ninth android and drew it backward so that the neck muscles were taut. He raised the knife.

Then he paused and looked down with a faint expression of interest in his otherwise empty eyes. "Are you afraid to die?"

"I don't—know. What is it to—die?"

"You become nonfunctioning."

"I think I would rather not become nonfunctioning."

The tenth android cut the ninth android's throat. Carefully

and cleanly, he severed the big artery that carried the blood-fluid back down to the upper heart.

The blood-fluid spouted out and drained down over the chest of the ninth android. He shuddered. His eyes closed. When the tenth android released his grip, the head fell forward.

And from somewhere in the synthetically created mind of the tenth android there came a question: Was it undesirable to become nonfunctioning? The human was afraid to die. He sensed this but not the reason for it, if there was one. The human was afraid to die.

He wondered only momentarily, vaguely recorded it as a mistake to wonder about such things, and then crossed the room and put the red-stained knife into the sink.

After that, he let himself quietly out of the apartment and walked off down the street.

He had much to do. He had to leave town and finish the project alone.

Then, quite suddenly, he stopped, stepped into a nearby doorway and stood motionless. There was no change in his expression except that possibly his eyes became a shade emptier.

After a while he left the doorway and moved on. But it was with new purpose and with new plans.

The new orders, relayed across a light-year of space, were not intercepted by any terrestrial receiving device, however sensitive. But they were received and recorded perfectly in the mind of the tenth android.

*****

Frank Corson and Les King sat in a coffee shop and regarded each other with a certain wariness. "It's like this, at least from where I sit," King said. "About ten years ago a small-town judge named Sam Baker—"

"You told me that," Corson cut in impatiently. "Baker was supposed to have been drowned, but they never found the body. Now, you think William Matson is Sam Baker?"

King pondered the question morosely. "I've got every right to think so. But Baker would have aged some in ten years. The man I saw—"

"The man you saw didn't have a broken leg. I must have seen the same one when I—"

King was instantly alert. When you were on the trail of ten grand you had to be alert, and suspicious of comparative strangers.

"You saw someone who looked like Baker and Matson? A guy without a broken leg?"

"I was leaving an apartment building on the Upper East Side this morning. I met him in the street."

"You didn't tell me that."

"I'm telling you now."

King scowled. "I don't get it. You were the doctor. You left a man with a broken leg in bed in a hospital. You saw a man who looked like—"

"I saw the same man, goddamn it!"

"All right—the same man. And you didn't do anything about it? You didn't say *Good morning* or *It might rain* or *What the hell are you doing out of bed?* You just let him walk away?"

"You're being unreasonable. When you come face to face with something that's impossible, you don't treat it as a fact. It throws you off balance."

King continued to scowl. "We're not getting anywhere. Let's face it. It *was* impossible. Let's get the hell up to your room and talk to William Matson."

"All right."

Frank Corson came half out of his chair, then he dropped back again. "I don't like this," he said.

"What's to like? What's to dislike? For ten thousand dollars we can ignore both."

"I have a feeling we're getting into something beyond our depth."

"Okay, then let me handle it. I'll see that you get your cut."

"Not so fast," Corson said sharply. "I didn't say I was backing out. I just said this might be bigger than we bargain for."

"I don't think that's quite it," King replied coldly. "I think you don't trust me."

"Maybe that's it. I don't think you trust me, either."

"Ten thousand *is* a lot of money. But we're not going to get it by sitting in a coffee shop arguing over it."

"I guess you're right."

"Then let's go."

They left the coffee shop and, as they walked the four blocks that separated them from the room where he was ashamed to take Rhoda Kane, Frank Corson analyzed his own mood and attitude. He decided it wasn't that he mistrusted King, or that he actually thought the deal had any frightening elements in it. In plain truth, he was ashamed of himself. Somehow, in his own mind, he was degrading his profession. His love of Rhoda Kane, his need of money, his impatience with time and circumstance, had forced him into what seemed like a cheap intrigue. There was, somehow, a bad taste to the whole thing.

But it was too late to back out now. And what the hell! If there was ten thousand dollars lying around, why shouldn't he get a piece of it? What was wrong with that? He unlocked the door to his room.

He took a step forward and stopped, blocking the entrance.

"Oh, my God!"

Les King pushed through. His eyes widened, but that was his only reaction. Then his camera swung up into position. The bulb flashed. He lowered the camera.

"Somebody cut the bastard's throat!" he marveled.

Frank Corson moved forward. "Good lord! It looks as though he just sat there and let himself be murdered."

"Suicide maybe?"

"No knife close enough. It's over there in the sink."

"Well, he didn't cut his own throat and then walk back here."

Frank Corson had been studying the wound. He pressed his fingers against the crimson shirt front and rubbed them together, testing the feel of the blood with his thumb.

"What's wrong?" King asked.

"I don't know. That's an odd color for coagulating blood. It doesn't feel right, either."

"Do you think he was sick?"

"There's just something crazy about this whole thing. The man had two hearts."

King was both amazed and angered. "What the hell are you talking about?"

"I didn't get a chance to tell you. This man was a freak. I found it out last night. He had two hearts. I'm sure of it."

"No chance to tell me? Why, goddamn it, we sat in that coffee shop for half an hour while I leveled with you. No chance! You held out on me." King laughed cynically. "I guess that's human nature. With a couple of bucks at stake even honest men go cagey."

Corson ignored the jibe. "Listen, for Christ sake! This is murder! Can't you understand that?"

"Of course, it's murder—in your room, with your knife. You'll have some explaining to do."

King's face hardened. He became subtly remote, impersonal. His eyes turned cold as he began inserting flash-bulbs into his camera and snapping the room and the body from various angles.

Frank Corson, out of his depth for sure now, stood helpless. Les King looked up from his work. "Well, don't just stand there, Doctor. You've got a murder to report. Get with it."

As Corson turned helplessly toward the door, King grinned faintly. "Me, I'm just a free-lance photographer trying to make an honest buck."

*****

Brent Taber stared icily down at Frank Corson and Les King. They looked up at him sullenly, looming over them as he did, from the position of authority. A little like two schoolboys being punished by the principal, they lowered their eyes. Defiantly, each told himself that he was a free citizen and didn't have to take this from Taber, even if he did represent governmental authority.

Still, they sat and took it.

"Of course," Taber said, "you have the universal alibi. You didn't know how serious this thing was. So far as you were concerned, you'd located a man with a reward on his head." He shook his head deprecatingly. "If we hadn't sent out a top-secret bulletin to all the big-city police chiefs to be on the lookout for this guy you'd have had it spread in some tabloid."

"A person has a right to make a buck," King said stubbornly.

"Oh, sure. Again the universal defense. Make the buck first and then think about your patriotic duty."

"Patriotic duty, hell! There wasn't any as far as I was concerned. When I found out about that—What the hell did you call him? The android?—he was already dead."

"And you'll do very well with the pictures you took."

"They're my pictures."

"The hell they are. We're confiscating them and you'll keep your mouth shut about this."

"Then the people haven't got a right to know—"

"Damn the people!" Brent snarled, and wished instantly that he hadn't said it. He didn't mean it, of course. He'd just been pressed too hard. In a sense, he was taking his own frustrations out on these two because they were handy.

And yet, damn it all, he was right! Nobody gave a hoot for the welfare of the country!

"You," he said, turning on Frank Corson. "In the course of

your duty as a doctor, you came upon something very strange."

"I wasn't sure!"

"You found a man with two hearts. What should you have done as a doctor? Reported it through recognized channels. If you'd done that, do you realize we might have got word? We might have been able to act? We might have saved that creature's life. That may well have been the difference between life and death for this country. For this planet."

"Are you sure you're not exaggerating things a little?" King asked the question and lit a cigarette as his self-confidence began to return. "Isn't the whole thing pretty far-fetched?"

Brent held his temper. "I suppose you have every right to assume we aren't really sure ourselves. But please listen to me now and give me the benefit of the doubt. We have reason to believe that these creatures—there have been others—are a menace to our survival. We're also pretty sure that there's another one roaming around. It's my opinion that the last one, the tenth one, may have had something to do with what happened in Dr. Corson's room. I don't know whether your lives are in danger or not, but *please* co-operate with us. Please report immediately anything of a suspicious nature that you see."

"Of course, we will," Frank Corson said. "I didn't see any signs of hostility in the other one, though."

"Be that as it may, we *must* get our hands on him."

"If he did kill the one with the broken leg," King said, "wouldn't he have left town?"

"If he thinks like a murderer, yes. But he probably doesn't. That's the trouble. We don't know how he thinks or what he's here for. We're playing it by ear."

"I think we understand," Frank Corson said.

"Thank you. And I'm sorry if I antagonized you. That wasn't my purpose. I'm just trying to do my job." He smiled and held out his hand. "This is all strictly confidential, of course."

"Of course."

"Thanks for coming."

They left, but Brent Taber's frustrations remained with him. Earlier that day, in Washington, he'd stood on the carpet himself, before higher authority, and played the part of the reprimanded schoolboy.

"It would appear," Authority said, "that you went out of your way to antagonize Senator Crane."

"I'm sorry if that's the opinion up above."

"It is not a matter of opinion, one way or another. It's a matter of expediency. The Administration has to get along with Congress. Senator Crane is in a powerful position. He is on three committees that can hamper legislation the Administration is vitally interested in."

"I understand. And I didn't pick the quarrel with Senator Crane. He picked it with me. In my judgment, he is not the kind of person to be trusted with information of this vital nature."

"You consider Senator Crane an unreliable demagogue?"

"I didn't say that."

Authority smiled wryly. "I'll concede that the Senator's type is rare in American politics—at least among those who get elected to high office. But the fact remains—he is a power."

"If you agree that the information should have been withheld—"

"I didn't agree on that at all," Authority said quickly. "And don't quote me as having said so. I'll deny it."

Brent Taber smiled also, but inwardly, where it wouldn't show. He should have expected that denial. After all, Authority had Higher Authority to account to. Authority could also be put on the carpet. There was always Someone higher up.

"I'm sorry," Brent Taber said. "I was put in charge of this project and I used my judgment—"

"We are not questioning your over-all judgment," Authority assured him.

Then what in the hell are you gabbling about? This question was also asked inwardly as Brent said, "I felt the gravity of the situation merited extreme care."

"It does. But life must go on. The government must still function."

That's right, play it from both ends, Brent Taber thought bitterly. Ride the fence. Stay in a position to jump either way.

"What do you wish me to do about Senator Crane?"

"I'd stay out of his way if I were you."

"Whatever damage you say I have done can be corrected with a ten-minute briefing."

"That's up to you," Authority answered nimbly. "As you say, you've been put in charge of the project."

"Then I'll leave things as they are."

"Very well. I just wanted to go on record."

"Thank you," Brent Taber said. "Thank you very much."
*****

Frank Corson and Les King walked north together after their interview with Brent Taber.

"I guess we got off lucky," King said. "Those Washington appointees can be tough."

"He seems to have a pretty tough job."

"They all think they've got tough jobs."

"It's still a murder as far as the New York police are concerned. What do you think will happen?"

"They turned us over to Taber, didn't they?" King asked. "That shows how they're playing it. The New York cops have enough murders to worry about. They like to pass them on to somebody else."

"Then they won't question us any further?"

King shrugged. "Who knows? You've got nothing to worry about, though. Just sit tight. In fact, you're damned lucky."

"How so?"

"This killing is under wraps. Nobody's talking. That means you won't get in trouble at the hospital." King grinned. "Your *ethics* won't come under scrutiny."

Frank Corson flushed and said nothing. King, after a moment's silence, said, "I've been thinking about that tenth android."

"Do you think there's as much danger in this thing as Taber says?"

King shrugged. "Those guys always think that way. Remember what they said about the atom bomb? The world was doomed. We were going to blow each other up. But nobody's been heaving them around. The view-with-alarm boys always talk that way."

"I hope you're right."

"But about that android that's supposed to be walking around loose."

"What about him?"

"Those bastards confiscated all my stuff. The shots I made in your room—everything. But if I could get some shots of the other one—"

"You're actually going to work on your own? In spite of what Taber said?"

"It's a free country," King retorted hotly. "I've got a right to follow my profession. What I was going to say was that you're in a position to help yourself a little, too."

"I am?"

"Only you and I know what we're looking for. If you spot the android, see him hanging around anywhere, and let me know, I'll—"

"You can go to hell, King. I want no part of any more of your ideas. I've had it. If I see the creature I'll call Taber and nobody else. I'm going to do exactly what he told me to do. Mark me off your list."

Frank Corson strode away. Les King stood watching him. King shrugged. Just another bewildered citizen who thought God lived in Washington. Afraid to spit if some Washington bureaucrat wagged a finger.

Well, the hell with Corson. The hell with Taber. The hell with all of them. If Les King stood to make an honest buck, he was going to do his damnedest until somebody passed a law making it illegal.

6

Brent Taber was drawn to Doctor Entman. He found, in the ugly little scientist, a rapport that seemed to exist nowhere else. At the moment, Entman was having a fine, stimulating time dissecting the cadaver of the android. His ugly little eyes were bright. "It's a miracle, my friend! A positive miracle. The thing these people have been able to do!"

"People? You've used that word before."

Entman waved an impatient hand. "Oh, don't quibble! Why, the creation of an artificial digestive system alone is awesome—not to mention the creation of a synthetic brain."

"The brain is what interests me."

"I can hardly wait to get into that area. Certain aspects are obvious, though. These creatures must have mental powers far beyond ours—in certain areas, that is."

"Tell me more."

"That's merely a matter of logic. We know that *homo sapiens*—because of his free choice, so to speak—uses, on an average, not more than a tenth of his mental ability. All right. These people have created, to all intents and purposes, a man. They surely had sense enough to remove the free-choice element. The creature surely has judgment, even cunning, but it is no doubt pointed totally and completely toward the objective of its being."

"Whatever the hell that objective is!"

Entman was mildly surprised by Taber's exclamation. He held up a warning finger. "Nerves, boy, nerves. You must watch that. As to the objective—I'm sure it's something pointed at our destruction."

"What powers were you referring to?"

"Hypnotism, I should think. Any of the mental processes through which one human being strives to assert control over another. We are aware of several of these. They may have found others."

"You won't be able to define them by cutting up that brain?"

"I doubt it. We could know them only by watching one of the creatures in action." Entman sighed. "If we only had other facts."

"What facts?"

Entman's smile was almost patronizing. "You're tired, aren't you, son? You're not thinking very well."

"Goddamn it! Quit treating me like a cretin!"

"Temper, temper! Look at it analytically, son, analytically. Suppose we knew who these people are. What distances have they covered in arriving here? What is their method of conveyance?"

"The distance? Light years, I would assume. The conveyance? A spaceship, or a projectile along basic lines but farther advanced."

"All right. We know they've sent ten creatures to our planet from infinity—that's as good a word to use as any. The next question is, why?"

"Damnit, that question is obvious."

"And from my point of view, the answer is obvious."

"Then I wish to hell you'd give it to me."

"Logic, man, logic! A race as far advanced as this one could certainly move in and occupy us without trouble. Wouldn't you think?"

"Certainly. That's what bothers me. Why all the pussy-footing around with synthetic men who keep dropping dead?"

"I think it's because they themselves are unable to exist in the climatic and atmospheric conditions existent on our planet."

Brent Taber's eyes opened as Entman went on. "They plan to occupy us, certainly—this we must assume—so they're trying to create an entity through which they can do it. The process is really no different, even though a little more dramatic, than our science creating a mechanical unit that functions to the best efficiency under specified conditions."

Taber's finger snapped up. He pointed at Entman's desk. "They'd like to know why their androids died. Maybe they weren't alike—at least, not exactly alike. Maybe there were differences you haven't found yet—maybe they turned out ten models and they want to know which one worked the best."

"You get the point," Entman beamed.

"They'd like the data you're assembling—those reports you've got in front of you."

"I imagine they'd find them quite interesting."

"Do you think we can assume the tenth android died also?"

"Perhaps. We have no proof that it killed the one found slain in Greenwich Village."

"I'm satisfied to assume that. But I'm wondering just what contact those 'people,' as you call them, had with their androids. Could a part of the brain have been a sending and receiving device?"

"It would be difficult to tell. I delved in far enough to find a mechanical device, if there had been one. It did not exist in those I dissected. There is another possibility though, except that we often make the mistake of assuming that what we humans on earth can't do, can't be done. Consider telepathy. Who's to say they were not made capable of communicating in that way—at whatever distance?" He paused for a moment, deep in thought, before going on. "Has it occurred to you that the tenth android might be a supervisor, the boss, the captain? If he is still alive, why haven't you found him? You have the men and facilities at your command."

Brent Taber sprang to his feet. "Doctor," he answered, scowling, "Did you ever hear of a project so secret that it couldn't even be given enough personnel to make it work?"

Entman smiled sympathetically. "Washington is a strange place in some ways, son. Usually it's the other way around. You get so much help they get in each other's way. I'm glad I'm not involved in those phases of it."

Brent paced the floor, occupied with his own thoughts. It was more than mere frustration. It went deeper. There was his resentment of the dressing-down he'd taken from Authority; the subtle coolness that had begun to permeate his relations with those upstairs.

He jerked his mind away from such thoughts. Nerves. That was it. He was tense. He was imagining things. They were certainly too well aware of the gravity of this situation to let petty politics interfere.

Or were they?

"Okay, Doc," Brent said crisply. "Thanks for letting me pick your brain."

"Good luck, son."

Entman went back to his work and Taber left. As he walked down the corridor, he analyzed the cheerful tone of Entman's voice and told himself that even Entman didn't really believe it. Entman had the evidence before his eyes but he still couldn't get the concept of alien creatures from space really taking us over. It was too unbelievable.

Am I the only one who really believes it? He asked himself this question as he hailed a cab in the street and watched a fat man in a bowler hat slip in and take it away from him.

"You're slipping, Taber," he muttered. "You're definitely slipping."

*****

The bell rang. Rhoda Kane opened the door. The man standing there was not extraordinary in any way. He appeared just short of middle age. He wore a blue suit and a blue necktie. The word for him was *quiet*. He was a man who did not stand out.

"My name is John Dennis," he said. "I would like to speak to you."

The abrupt demand annoyed Rhoda. She frowned and was about to retort just as peremptorily, but an odd bemusement tempered her mood. The man was uncivil enough to be interesting. She said, "I'm busy now," but instead of closing the door, she stepped back into the room. The man came in and it was he who closed the door.

"I don't wish to alarm you, Miss Kane."

"I'm not in the least alarmed."

As she spoke, Rhoda wondered if this was true. But the wondering itself was on such an impersonal basis that it didn't seem to make much difference.

Also, she was noticing that John Dennis was not quite as he'd first appeared. He was much younger than middle-aged, really—somewhere in his thirties. He was quiet, yes, but handsome, too. There was a rugged individuality about him that was easily missed at first glance. A definite attractiveness.

"I want to ask you about a friend of yours. Frank Corson."

This seemed like a logical request. It definitely seemed that way but, at the same time, Rhoda was confused as to why it should appear to be. A man came and knocked on the door and entered and asked a question like that. It *shouldn't* have been all right, but it was. He probably had the right, she told herself, else he would not have asked.

"What do you wish to know?"

"Tell me about him."

"He is a doctor. Frank is an intern at Park Hill Hospital. After he finishes there he will go into practice. I guess that's about all there is to it."

"He had a patient named William Matson."

"William Matson? I don't know. He doesn't discuss his work with me."

"This was a patient with a broken leg who was taken to the hospital night before last."

"He did mention one man. I don't know his name, though. A man Frank said had two hearts."

"What else did he tell you about this man?"

"Nothing else. Frank had the case in Emergency. We came home—came here—and then Frank was bothered. He went back and examined the man and came out and said he had two hearts."

"That was all he said?"

"Nothing else."

John Dennis looked around. Then, when Rhoda stirred and passed a hand quickly through her hair, he brought his eyes back to bear on hers. Rhoda lowered her hand.

"Does Frank Corson live here?"

"No. This is my home. Frank lives in the Village."

"What Village?"

"Greenwich Village. It's a part of New York. Are you a stranger?"

John Dennis did not answer. "Why doesn't he live here with you?"

"Why—why, we're not married. We are only engaged."

"That means you will get married later?"

"I hope to."

"Does he hope to?"

"Yes—I'm sure he does."

"Then he will live here with you?"

"I don't know. We may find another place."

"What's wrong with this one?"

"Why, nothing—nothing at all—"

Such strange questions, Rhoda thought. Why was he asking them? No doubt he had a reason. It somehow did not occur to her to wonder why she was answering. Her own thoughts on the matter did not seem important.

"He lives here with you sometimes, doesn't he?"

"He stays over once in a while."

"Why doesn't he stay over all the time?"

"Because we're not married."

"What do you do when he stays over?"

"We—talk."

"Is that all?"

"We make love."

"How do you do that?"

Rhoda hesitated for the first time. "We—haven't you ever

made love?"

His words came a little sharper. "How do you make love?"

"We lie in each other's arms. We show affection for each other."

"You lie in the same bed together?"

"Yes. Of course."

"If you were married, what would you do?"

"I said—we would live together."

"Would you make love?"

"Yes."

"Would you lie in the same bed together?"

"Yes."

"Is there anything you would do if you were married that you don't do now?"

"Of course. We would live together. We would be man and wife. It would be—well, legal."

"It is not legal to make love and lie in the same bed together now?"

"No—well, yes—you see—"

He was joking, of course. Rhoda was sure of this. She wanted to explain it all to him but he suddenly lost interest.

"Frank Corson knew nothing else about William Matson?"

"The man with two hearts?"

"Only that?"

"It was all he told me."

"I think he knows more. I want you to ask him. Then I will come and ask you."

"I'll ask him if he knows anything more than what he told me."

"Ask him if he knows of any other men with two hearts. I want to know where they are and what happened to them."

"I'll try to find out."

"You *must* find out."

"Will you come back soon?"

"I will come back. You must do as I tell you."

"I will do as you tell me."

John Dennis had been sitting by the window so that Rhoda had to stare into the light. He got up and approached her. She stood up and waited for him, motionless. He came close and looked at her curiously. His eyes went up and down her body. He laid a hand on her left breast and pressed gently. She did not move.

"I will come back. You will not tell anyone I have been here or that we talked." He left without saying good-bye.

After he was gone, Rhoda stood where she was, motionless, for several minutes. Her mind was on the place he had touched her. She had never before experienced such a reaction. Never before had a man's hand, even on her bare flesh, produced such thrill and excitement. Desperately, her common sense struggled with this new thing. She dismissed with annoyance the callow, schoolgirl thought that this was the way love finally came—in the door, unannounced, to take over a woman's heart and soul and body. Ridiculous.

The intellectual Rhoda agreed, but the emotional Rhoda continued to toy with the idea, finding it a fascination, a joy. But there was something more than the intellectual and the emotional; a deeper, frightening numbness; a strange paralysis of mind she could not come to grips with; it kept eluding her even as she reached out for it.

Fear? She wondered.

But mainly she thought of John Dennis, the strange man who had walked in her door and to whom she had surrendered without a struggle.

My God. What happened to me? What happened to Rhoda Kane?

Abruptly she dropped the thought—it did not seem important.

*****

Senator Crane sat in the dining room of the Mayflower Hotel. His guest was Matthew Porter, a mystery man, also, of the Brent Taber type, but a little more clearly defined in that he had a title and a department of government. But far more important to Crane, he outranked Taber.

One other point of importance: Matthew Porter was, in the terms even Senator Crane used, "something of a fathead."

"Maybe I am a Senator," Crane said jovially, "and maybe we boys up there think we have a hand in directing you fellows—still I'm flattered that you could find time to lunch with me."

Porter had a thin, aristocratic face, delicate features. His expression was usually benign, but there was steel behind it. He could scowl and hurl righteous invective, for instance, when a policeman questioned his right to park by a fireplug in spite of his official license plates.

But mainly he was a shy person who nursed his inferiority complex in secret.

"That's very flattering, Senator. But the truth is quite the opposite. It's we fellows who are honored to put ourselves at your beck and call. After all, you're the ones the people elect to office."

The flattery boomeranged nicely and put Porter one up on Crane.

"The people must be served, of course," Crane said, "and that's one of the things I want to talk to you about. The people's interests."

Matthew Porter cocked an alarmed eye as he bit into a roll. "Have their interests been violated?"

Crane glanced around and lowered his voice. "There's been too much loose talk going around about that project you've got Brent Taber on."

Porter laid the roll down very carefully, as though he feared it might go off. "I'm not sure I know what you're referring to, Senator."

"Your reticence is quite understandable. That I bring it up at all must shock you, but—" Crane hesitated, a touch of sadness brushing across his face.

"But what, Senator?"

"You understand, certainly, that I hold the greatest respect for Brent Taber. That's why I hesitated to come to you."

"It seems to me Halliday said something about calling Taber in. It had to do with a mild reprimand over Taber's attitude on legislative-executive relations."

"Halliday?" Senator Crane asked innocently. "He's another of the really good men you picked for government service."

"I trust Halliday implicitly, but he's carrying a big load so I'm glad you came directly to me, Senator. Exactly what is the trouble?"

"In plain words, there have been some bad leaks out of Taber's office. There is in existence a taped recording of a meeting."

Porter was aghast. He tried to hide it, which made his greenish expression all the more ludicrous—as though he'd swallowed a worm out of his salad.

"Impossible."

"You'd think so, with all the top-secret precautions that have been taken."

"How did you discover this?"

Crane held up a restraining hand. "I'd be happy to tell you if it would serve any purpose, but believe me, it wouldn't. I would only tend to eliminate a contact who is extremely loyal to me and—I might add—to good government."

"I understand. But I certainly can't imagine what has happened to Taber. I would have backed him with my last dime."

"I actually don't think it was Taber's fault. A man can't personally see to every detail in his department."

"That's the responsibility of whoever is in charge."

Crane sighed. "Yes, I guess that's a cold, hard fact of life in this time of danger. But don't be too hard on him. Perhaps there's an explanation."

"He'll have his chance to explain," Porter said grimly.

"I'm sure you understand how it pains me to have to—well, put this black mark on the record of a good man. I debated many hours and searched my soul before I came to you. With a man's career at stake—"

"Men are expendable," Porter snapped. "The nation's safety is not."

Again Crane glanced around. "Are the Russians *really* that far ahead?"

Porter's eyes narrowed just a shade. "The Russians? Did you listen to the tape you mentioned?"

"Only sketchily. I assumed—"

"The danger is far greater. A Senatorial committee was briefed on the thing. I honestly think you should have been on that committee, Senator. By coming to me you've done far more toward protecting the nation's safety—and that of the world—than have any of your colleagues."

"Let's just say I had more opportunity."

"Your modesty is becoming."

"And now," Crane said wryly, "now that I've done all I can, I wish I could forget the whole thing. But with the gravity of the situation—"

"I'll see that you get a complete briefing."

"Thank you. And I promise I'll be most discreet."

A little while later, on the way back to his office, Crane smiled. Now maybe that self-important little son-of-a-bitch, Taber, would find out what it meant to insult a United States Senator.

From there, his mind went to another insult. So they'd passed him up in forming the committee to hear about the damned androids, had they? Well, by God, he'd show them the people of his state wouldn't tolerate that, either.

The people back home were going to hear about their Senator.

It probably wouldn't even be necessary to campaign next year.

7

"If you've changed your mind about anything—about us, maybe—just say so. I'll understand." Frank Corson felt he had to make this point—at this particular time. There was something inevitable in the need to do so.

"You're being ridiculous. The old thing about money again," Rhoda parried.

"There's nothing old about money. The problem is ever new. It's always with us."

Rhoda Kane wanted to cry. She sat on the floor beside the sofa on which Frank Corson lay, his hands behind his head, his eyes staring up at the ceiling. She wanted to say, *Darling, what's happened to me? What is this thing inside me that keeps blocking me away from you? Why can't I tell you about it?*

But she could not say this. She could only push the tears back and lay her head seductively on his chest. "You're just tired, dear. You've been working too hard."

He ran his hand petulantly through her hair. "It isn't me. It's you, Rhoda. Half the time you don't even realize I'm talking to you. You're getting such a faraway look in your eyes I'm beginning to think there's another man."

"That's silly," she said lightly. "Let me make you a drink."

"I don't want a drink."

The way he responded to her kiss indicated he didn't want to make love, either. Rhoda settled back to the floor and said, "Darling—"

Suddenly she couldn't go on. Somewhere inside, a dam broke; the strange, bewildering block tottered and began to fall. "Darling—there's something I want to tell you—"

Frank Corson indicated with a jerk of his head. "The phone's ringing."

"Let it ring. Darling, I—"

"For heaven's sake, answer it, Rhoda. It might be important."

She got up, went to the phone and picked it up. "Hello."

"This is John Dennis."

She felt that frightening excitement again—that feeling of dangerous delight at something forbidden. "Yes?"

"Do you remember what I told you to do?"

"Yes."

"Has it been done?"

"Not yet."

"Why have you not done it?"

"I haven't had a chance."

"You have a chance now. Frank Corson is in your home."

"Yes. I have a chance now."

The phone clicked. Rhoda put it down and went back to the sofa. As she sank to the floor, Frank Corson looked at her questioningly.

"That was certainly a cryptic conversation."

When Rhoda didn't answer, he scowled and snapped, "There you go again. Into the brown study."

"Oh, I'm sorry, dear."

"What was the phone call about?"

"My hairdresser. It was nothing."

"Weird conversation to have with a hairdresser."

"He's a weird hairdresser."

"What had you started to say when the phone rang?"

"It just occurred to me—you never told me what happened when that government man talked to you."

Frank wished she hadn't brought that up. He'd been ordered to keep the incident in his room strictly to himself. That hadn't been too difficult. It *had* been hard not to look on the thing as a murder. The blood had looked real and so had the body.

But if that was the way Brent Taber wanted it, all right. Frank was amazed at how smoothly everything had been handled. There hadn't even been a police car at the door—just an unmarked delivery truck and two men carrying out what might have been a rolled-up rug.

And that had been that.

"He didn't say much. Actually, there was no point in mentioning it to you."

"What ever happened to the man with two hearts?"

"I was wrong. He just had a peculiar heartbeat. As a matter of fact, everybody's heart beats all over their body. Nothing strange about that."

"But there's something strange about a doctor not being able to tell the difference between one heart and two. Frank, you *are* keeping something from me."

"Rhoda! For heaven's sake! The government man told me to keep my mouth shut about it."

"Does that mean you can't tell even me?"

He turned his head and looked into her eyes. "This isn't like you, Rhoda. Not like you at all."

"That's silly. I haven't changed."

"Yes, you have."

"How?"

"It's hard to say. You don't seem to have the same sense of values any more. You've—"

"Just how have they changed?"

If he sensed any inner fright in her question he said nothing about it. "For instance, when I told you I'd given up all ideas of going into research, when I said I'd decided to finish out my internship and establish a practice, you hardly twitched an eyebrow. I thought that would make you happy."

"It did, darling. I was delighted. But I'm still a woman and that gives me a right to be curious. What *did* the government man say?"

He sighed and drew her cajoling hand out of his hair. "They've got some wild idea the man who broke his leg wasn't a man at all. They think he was a synthetic of some kind. An android."

"Why, that's ridiculous. You saw him. You certainly know a man when you see one."

"According to Brent Taber, these androids *are* men, to all intents and purposes, but they're manufactured."

"That's just utterly insane. Are we paying taxes just to keep a lot of people in Washington who don't know the difference between a human being and a—"

"Rhoda! Please! I'm sick of the whole thing and I'd rather not talk about it."

"But he must have told you more than that. Where do these— these androids come from?"

"He didn't tell us any more than he had to, but I got the idea they think they're from outer space."

Rhoda laughed. "I never heard such foolishness in my life." She stopped laughing abruptly. "Who's *us*?"

"What?"

"You said, 'He didn't tell *us* any more than he had to . . .' Who was with you?"

"Oh. Les King. You don't know him."

She seemed satisfied with the information and probed no farther.

He drew her close and looked very seriously into her eyes. "You have changed, Rhoda. What's got into you?"

She put her lips to his and whispered, "Is this changed?" She ran one hand softly and seductively down his body. "Or that?"

He took her in his arms. "No, baby, that hasn't changed. I guess I was wrong."

And as she kissed him, she saw the oddly expressionless face, the cold empty eyes—of John Dennis.

And she was afraid.

*****

Something in the mind that had been given him—the synthetic duplicate of what had once been a part of Sam Baker—told the tenth android that women were attractive. For just what reason, he could not tell. There was nothing in his practical working structure that had any need of women. Still, the attraction was there in the memory patterns that had been transferred.

There were other attractions just as puzzling to him. He had vague memories of people with whom he felt no affinity except as vaguely nostalgic memories—Sam Baker's mother, his father, the blurred faces of friends he had known. And, at times, there were faint tinges of the terror Sam had known that night when a quick light flashed down from nowhere and he was abducted into a world too strange and terrible to be real. Yet it *had* been real.

There were no birth memories in the android, but there were the vestiges of Sam's death memories: the endless torture under a machine so sensitive that, while it had no definition of a woman, it was able to discern—in the names thefted from Sam's memory and used as names for the ten androids—those which applied to males and those that did not.

But of all these traces of memories, those concerning women nagged the android most. And now, as it turned his empty gaze on Rhoda Kane, it was with a little more personal interest than before.

"What did Frank Corson tell you?"

"He said the man in the hospital with a broken leg was not a man. He was an android."

The term, grotesquely enough, meant nothing to the creature who called himself John Dennis. In the strange pattern of his consciousness there were no patterns of definitive difference. Though in many respects more able than the humans against whom he was pitted, he was no more aware of himself as different than a dog is aware of its differences from a man. The concept didn't take shape in the android's synthetic mind.

"Did he tell you where the man with the broken leg came from?"

"He said they thought it came from somewhere in outer space."

"There were others. Did he know of them?"

"No. He only told me about a man named Les King."

"What did he say about Les King?"

"King was there when the government man talked to Frank. That was all. The government wanted them to say nothing."

"But Frank Corson told you."

"He would not tell anyone else, though. He is not interested in the androids. He wants to forget them."

"But Les King does not want to forget them?"

"I don't know."

"Will he talk about them?"

"I don't know that, either. I have never seen Les King."

"Can the government man keep Les King from talking about the man with the broken leg?"

"I doubt if he can force him to."

John Dennis again left the window and approached Rhoda Kane. She was wearing a housecoat, a brassiere and panties underneath.

"Take off your clothes."

Rhoda unbuttoned the housecoat and slipped it off. That strange excitement showed in her eyes now.

The android pointed. "Take those off."

As she unhooked her brassiere, Rhoda said, "My head aches."

"Your head does not ache."

"You are right, my head does not ache."

She slipped out of the panties and stood naked. The android regarded her. "You are different."

"Of course. I am a woman."

"I want to make love." As Rhoda stood motionless, helpless, he spoke very positively. "You make love on the bed. We will go into the bedroom . . ."

Later, she was never able to recall any details of that next half-hour. In defense of her own sanity, she was able to block the incident from her mind. But as she lay naked on the bed, looking up at the man she knew as John Dennis, she thought of her mind as being in two sections. One section, the part of her consciousness that clung to reality, kept saying, *I want to cry. If I could cry, everything would be all right. Why can't I cry?*

The other part was a pool of quivering excitement. She lay motionless, watching John Dennis undress, garment by garment, until he, too, was naked.

His body was not perfect, yet it had an individual perfection of its own in Rhoda's eyes. The skin was smooth and white, the legs and hips firm and masculine. The chest was broad and Rhoda wanted to put her hands on it and feel John Dennis' hands on her own body.

He stood looking at her, a little like a child, she thought tenderly; a child waiting to be told what to do. She did not account this as strange—only as a shyness in him. She held out her arms.

He lowered himself onto the bed beside her. She put her arms around him and pressed her lips to his. She waited. Nothing happened.

He was neither cold nor passionate. He was neither hostile nor friendly. He was nothing.

"You wanted to make love," Rhoda whispered. "Here I am. Take me. Take me."

Instead, he disengaged himself, raised himself up on his elbows and looked down at her. "You are quite different."

She did not know whether to be complimented or offended. "I'm about the same as every other woman."

"You are different than I am."

"Of course I'm different." Was he joking? He didn't seem to be. He was deadly serious as he began examining her breasts.

This is mad. This is insane. Why can't I cry?

But the other part of her mind quivered with her body as John Dennis went over it, inch by inch. He appeared to be trying to memorize it. She moved and turned as his hands directed, a new kind of fire rising within her. She waited. He touched her and waited for a response. There was none; nor any feeling within her at that moment except the strange fire inside and the ache of her taut groin tendons.

John Dennis touched her again and noted the sudden jerk and quiver of her response. He became grotesquely, academically interested. He touched the same nerve surface again and studied her face for the response.

Her eyes were closed and her lower lip was gripped in her

teeth. "No," she gasped. "Not that way. Not that way—please."

She could have been pleading with a brick wall. John Dennis continued—her natural reactions interested him. He frowned and seemed puzzled by the excitement he generated within her.

Then she cried out and rolled away from him and lay sobbing, her face buried in the pillow. But they were dry sobs; strange, tense sounds filling a questionable and dubious ecstasy.

"You are cruel," she whimpered.

"Cruel?"

"You make love so brutally."

He considered this and then got off the bed. "I do not like making love."

He began putting on his clothes. She watched him, completely defeated. "Where do you come from?" she demanded. "Who are you? Why did you want to know about the man with the broken leg?"

He turned from putting on his shirt and stood motionless, looking down into her eyes and after a moment or two it did not matter to Rhoda again. It mattered no more than it had in the beginning. The strange fire had not been quenched by what had occurred. It was still there, in her mind more than in her body, but finding its boundaries was not important either.

"Are you going?"

"Yes."

"Will you come back?"

"I will come back. I want you to find out from Frank Corson what happened to the androids."

"He doesn't know."

"Have him find out for you."

"I can't do that."

"Then I will not come back."

Somehow, in the part of Rhoda Kane's mind that was beyond her control, the thought that John Dennis might not return took on the proportions of a disaster. Her feeling was akin to panic as she said, "I will make him find out."

"Then I will come back."

"Please. I will wait for you."

*****

Les King answered the knock on the door and broke into a smile. "Well, talk about luck! I've been looking all over hell for you. Come in. Come in."

The tenth android was already in. He walked across the room and turned to look back at Les King with the outside light behind him.

King returned the gaze and wondered if he was afraid. It was an odd thing to wonder about. A man should know his own emotions. But King could not quite analyze the ones that struck him at that moment. For one thing, he'd discounted most of what Taber had said. There was something going on here, true—something big. When the government could cover up a murder in Greenwich Village, there had to be a big score at stake. And there *had* been a murder—but no cops, no police cars, nothing. Only a couple of guys in an unmarked truck walking out with what could have been a rolled-up carpet. They'd swiped *his* pictures and told him to keep his mouth shut.

This last was what made Les King mad. He'd found the story. It was his by every right. But when they were ready to break it they'd do it through some privileged Washington newspaperman who'd get it on a silver platter. The hell with that stuff. It would take more than a shadowy character like Brent Taber to scare him off.

He looked at the man in the blue suit and said, "You've been lucky. They're after you."

"Who is *they*?"

"Taber. The government crowd. The police, too, maybe. You killed that guy in the Village, didn't you?" Les King had decided a bold approach was the best way. But he was no fool. He kept his hand on the doorknob and watched the man carefully. "By the way, you haven't told me your name."

"John Dennis."

"You look like a man named Sam Baker. He disappeared about ten years ago—from a little town upstate."

"I am John Dennis."

King shrugged. "Okay, you're John Dennis. All I want to do is stay on top of this thing and have the inside track when it breaks."

"Brent Taber told you to forget about it."

King did not like the odd feeling of helplessness that seemed to have a grip on him. He was not alarmed, though. Over and above this was a sense of excitement. There was money here—he knew damned well there was money here.

"You want money, don't you?"

The question startled King. Could the guy read his mind?

"Who the hell doesn't?" he retorted defensively. "If you're heeled you've got it made."

Somehow King felt that the pressure, the odd excitement, lessened in intensity. His nerves, he conceded, were sure playing tricks.

"There are some things I want. I will tell you where they are. I will give you money for them."

An espionage approach? King wondered. In a way, he hoped it was. He could always get clear. When the time was right, when he had the story locked, he'd go to the FBI with it. He had a quick vision of a spread in *Life*, a title: "I Broke the Russian Spy Ring." His own by-line.

"That sounds touchy," he said.

"I will tell you where to go and what to do."

"I'll have to know more than that."

"I will tell you what to do."

John Dennis left without saying good-bye.

Les King stared at the inner side of the closed door. "Jesus!" he muttered.

But the excitement was creeping back.

8

Brent Taber stood in front of the desk of Authority and said, "Mr. Porter, I don't think you people realize the gravity of this situation."

Porter's eyes were frosty. "And just what gives you that idea?"

"The fact that I'm being hamstrung at every turn. Men I assigned to search out the last android have been taken off the job, transferred away from me without notice."

"You speak of being *hamstrung*." Porter pronounced the term with an inflection of disgust, as though it were a vulgarism no gentleman would use. "You say we do not realize the gravity of the situation. Perhaps we realize it far more than you do. It may be that your activities have been indirectly curtailed because you have not recognized the vital need of harmony in government."

"Are you telling me Crane's ego is still smarting?"

"*Senator* Crane did, in the spirit of co-operation, mention certain leaks in your department."

"What in hell are you talking about?"

"I'd watch my tone if I were you, Taber. You aren't talking to one of your legmen now!"

Taber's teeth came tight together. "I'm sorry. Let me repeat the question. Exactly what was the nature of the leak to which the Senator referred?"

"A tape—transcribed at one of your top-secret meetings."

Taber's fist closed and opened. "I guess maybe I have been lax," he said softly.

Porter, grimly happy to have made his point, went on. "As to policy up above, I'll be quite frank. We have not necessarily gone along with your theory that the so-called androids were from outer space."

"Then where do you think they originated?"

"We have put data into the calculators on that point. So far, the results have been inconclusive."

"That's too bad."

"Your sarcasm is uncalled for. I am quite willing to tell you, however, that we have been proceeding in the matter. You are aware, no doubt, of the recent space shot that ended disastrously?"

"Who isn't?"

Still insistent upon treating Taber like a backward child,

Porter said, "The missile was safely launched and made five orbits and then suffered destruction."

"There was a lot of newspaper copy written on the failure; a lot of questions asked as to the cause."

"The releases were entirely true," Porter said with prim severity. "There was malfunction of crucial units under stress. But another phase was not made public. The astronaut's mission—one of them, at least—was to hunt outer space for foreign bodies of any description."

"What did he report?"

"Nothing."

"I recall a story printed by some Washington columnist that some of the code picked up from the missile was not translated for the press. This, he stated, in view of the Administration's current 'Open End' policy on such matters, was strange."

"If you're implying that we censored certain information, that's quite true. In the public interest."

"To keep scientific information out of Russian hands?"

"In this case, no. The astronaut fell victim to a psychological stress that was unforeseen. What he sent made no sense whatever. We blame the medical men for not finding the flaw in his psyche."

"And I would be entirely out of line in assuming he did discover hostile foreign bodies and was destroyed by them?"

"Entirely," Porter snapped.

Brent Taber's eyes were stony. "But I *am* to assume that you're asking for my resignation."

Now Porter shrugged. "If that is the way you see it, I can, of course, only tender my regrets."

"Well, you won't have to. I'm not resigning."

The sharp declaration made Porter blink. "It's rather unusual that a man, after a vote of no confidence—"

"To hell with that. If a tape got out of my office, it's my fault. I'll grant that. But there's more to this. I'm willing to bet the man who told you was the same one who engineered the steal."

"That's ridiculous! Are you accusing Senator Crane of—?"

"I'm accusing an opportunist-demagogue of playing fast and loose with national safety to further his own ends and salve his ego. I'm accusing the men above me of being too weak-kneed to back their own against outside interference."

"I'll stand for no insults from you, Taber!"

"You'll take it and like it," Brent Taber said savagely. "You'll take it because you can't knock me out of my office overnight. It will take time. You've got to go up through the command and you'll have to go pretty high before you'll find anyone who'll do it with the stroke of a pen. Nobody wants to stick their neck out."

"Of course," Porter replied icily, "if you care to keep functioning as a discredited person—"

"I can. And I will. I'd be a coward if I didn't."

Porter was obviously disappointed but he shrugged. "That's your privilege. You, of course, will not be taken off the payroll."

"The payroll be damned. Send my checks to the Red Cross!"

And Brent Taber strode out of Porter's office, a man who stood alone in the Washington jungle of clashing ambitions, of purposes and cross-purposes—but a man who had no thought of quitting.

After Brent left, Porter put through a call to Senator Crane's office.

". . . so, while severing Brent Taber from official activity would be rather difficult, Senator, I have, in the interests of efficiency, withdrawn most of his facilities."

"A wise move, Porter. A very wise move."

"By the way, Senator, that hydroelectric project on the Panamint River your Conservation people have in the works. I'm quite interested in it."

"Is that so?" Crane asked guardedly.

"Yes. Perhaps because of my experience along those lines in South America. I consider it a great opportunity to serve and I understand the administrator's post is still open."

Porter's tone was vague. "Yes. I believe it is."

"Of course, I'm quite happy where I am, you understand. I'm not looking for a change. However, the challenge does intrigue me."

"I'll give you a ring, Porter. Just sit tight until you hear from me."

After hanging up, Porter sat back and wondered. He tried to analyze the tone in which Crane had made the promise to call. It had been falsely cordial, beyond a doubt. Maybe Crane figured Taber's scalp was too small a price to pay for the hydroelectric plum. Well, in that case, Porter philosophized, he hadn't lost a great deal. It was all in the game.

*****

Frank Corson was confused and troubled by the changes that

continued to come over Rhoda Kane. He could not quite put his finger on the start of it, but as he saw her now, a scant two weeks after the incident of the man with two hearts, he could clearly see the changes. Where she had been a beautiful, poised, self-controlled woman, she was now more nervous and quick of movement, brighter of eye, full of a new restless energy he could not account for.

Also, the dominance in their affair had shifted. He had always, it seemed, been the dominant factor, in that Rhoda had continually catered to his moods and bent to the winds of his own unrest and dissatisfaction.

But one evening when he was free of duty at Park Hill, Rhoda came home and entered the apartment without glancing toward the double-width sofa by the window. Frank, stretched out with a drink in his hand, watched her as she took her key out of the lock and put it back in her purse. He was struck by the fact that with this new "personality" that had become a part of her, she was even more attractive than before. A glow had been added. The quiet, dignified, statuesque beauty of before had been mysteriously vitalized by a new kind of inner life.

She turned from the door and, looking into the bright glare of the eight-foot windows, she saw him on the sofa and took a quick step forward.

"Oh," she cried. "It's you!"

"Of course, it's me."

Rhoda stopped dead and Frank was sure that the look of eagerness died as suddenly as it had been born.

"Well, good lord! Whom were you expecting?"

Rhoda laughed. "You just surprised me, that's all."

"Well, you gave me the keys to your apartment. Wasn't I supposed to use them?"

"Of course, silly." She came across the room and sat down on the sofa beside him. She bent down and kissed him.

"Golly," he said, sarcastically enthusiastic, "that was about as stimulating as a meeting between two dead fish."

"Frank! For heaven's sake! What's got into you lately?"

"I think that question should be reversed. 'What's got into *you*?'"

"I think you're being unreasonable."

"Am I? Is it unreasonable to wonder why you did a complete about-face?"

"I don't understand."

"You understand. I've brought it up before. You spent weeks convincing me I ought to carry through with my internship and establish a practice. You said the time element didn't make any difference to you. You talked me out of the silly idea I had about cashing in on the man with two hearts. I admitted it was a silly idea. I turned away from it completely. Then you did the world's fastest about-face and began asking questions. You began pushing me in the direction you'd been arguing against."

Rhoda refused to match his serious mood. She ran a playful hand through his hair. "A woman has a right to change her mind, hasn't she?"

"Oh, stop it, Rhoda. You're avoiding the issue."

"All right. I still maintain I have a right to change my mind, but in making it all seem completely unnatural you neglected to mention *why* you changed yours. Because a man named Brent Taber slapped your wrist like a little boy and scared you. It wasn't my influence that turned you around and started you walking the other way. It was a *big* man from Washington who said naughty, naughty and suddenly you were a nice little intern again, afraid to ask questions."

"It was more dangerous than you know, Rhoda."

"Oh, I'm sure it was. Do you want another drink?"

"No." Frank looked out the window and scowled. "Rhoda, there was something I didn't tell you about that affair."

"Was there? I'll bet you told Brent Taber, though."

"It was what brought Brent Taber into it. There was a murder in my room."

"And when Brent Taber came on the scene—" Rhoda stopped and stared down at him. "What did you say?"

"A man was killed in my room. The man with the broken leg. He didn't just go on his way, as I told you; he got his throat cut in my room."

Rhoda continued to stare. "And you didn't tell me about it."

"Brent Taber told me to keep my mouth shut."

"I suppose if Brent Taber had said, 'I don't want you to see that woman again,' you wouldn't even have dropped around to say good-bye."

"Rhoda—you're being unreasonable."

"Unreasonable to expect the man who says he loves me to confide in me?"

"All right. I was wrong. What happened is this: When William Matson was ready to leave Park Hill, he had no place to go, so I took him down to my room. I went back to the hospital and Les King contacted me. He said William Matson was really a man named Sam Baker who'd disappeared from his home in upstate New York ten years ago. We went down to see him and found him sitting in a chair with his throat cut."

"You've been involved in a murder and you didn't say a single, solitary word—"

"Rhoda! I said I was sorry."

"I didn't see anything about it in the papers. I'm sure it wasn't on any of the newscasts."

"Of course, it wasn't. The police didn't even question me. I called the police and they came—two prowl-car men. Then they told Les and me to wait. We waited, and after a while this Brent Taber came in. He told us to go home and keep our mouths shut. Later, we were called downtown and Taber talked to us."

"He told you to go home," Rhoda said sarcastically. "You also said the man was killed in your room. Just where is your home, Mr. Corson?"

"I came here, Rhoda. I spent that night here."

"With a possible murder charge hanging over your head, you came here and didn't say a word!"

Frank sprang up from the couch and turned, scowling. "God-damn it! Don't you believe me? Do you think I'm lying?"

"I don't know what to believe. I just feel—betrayed. But something else is more important."

"What?"

"You acted like a child. Just because some man appeared out of nowhere, you said *Yes, sir* and *No, sir* and *Sorry, sir* and walked away. Frank! I'm ashamed of you!"

In quick anger, his hand came back as though to slap her. But he dropped it to his side and strode across the room and picked up his jacket.

"And so now you're walking out again. You just can't face up to anything, can you, Doctor Corson."

He turned on her, his eyes blazing. "All right. Maybe everything you say is true. Maybe I've seesawed and acted like a kid. If I have, it's because of you. The thing in the Village had nothing to do with me changing my mind about going into research. I did it because I thought you wanted me to."

Now Rhoda was on her feet, too, her patrician nostrils flaring. "Well, don't do me any favors."

"From now on, I wouldn't dream of it."

As he pulled on his jacket, Rhoda sat down on the sofa and lit a cigarette. "I'm convinced that if you'd gone along with Les King you would have been on the right road. King wasn't frightened off by a man who said he represented the government. He saw a chance to make some money and is probably going ahead with it right now."

"I don't give a damn what Les King is doing!"

"Of course not. But there's another little thing you overlooked. Don't you suppose this Brent Taber will toss that murder right back into your lap if it suits his purpose? The body was in your room. You're probably the chief suspect. So you sit back and let Brent Taber play whatever game he's got in mind. And if it goes wrong, Frank Corson gets picked up for murder."

"It can't possibly happen that way."

"Why not? Who is Brent Taber, really?"

"I told you—a government man."

"What government? Where can you get in touch with him?"

"I don't know. He gave me a phone number in case I ever saw a certain man again."

"What man?"

"Rhoda! They aren't men at all. They're androids!"

Rhoda froze and stared at him in consternation. "You actually *believe* that fairy tale? Frank, I just don't understand you."

"I told you about it before."

"But for the life of me I didn't think you took it seriously."

"I just didn't care. I'd had it. I wanted out."

"But you're involved in it, up to your neck, and if you had any guts you'd face Taber and make him tell you *all* the facts—and what's behind them."

"I have no intention of calling him."

"I guess that's the rock we split on then," Rhoda said coldly. She couldn't understand herself, even while she knew, deep down, that she wanted more information for *him*—John Dennis. Any other reason or excuse she used was a sham, a self-delusion.

If she expected a protest, she didn't get it. Rhoda took a long, calm drag on her cigarette. She ground it into the ash tray. She raised her eyes and looked levelly at Frank.

"Very well," he said, finally, "It was nice knowing you."

"Shut the door quietly on the way out," she retorted.

He stared at her, his face revealing nothing. He turned, went to the door, and opened it. He looked back. She had not moved. He left without a word.

Rhoda Kane lit another cigarette. She stared out across the East River at the expensive view that went with her high-rent apartment. She got up and went to the liquor cabinet and made herself a drink.

She was back on the sofa when a key turned in the lock. The door opened. Frank Corson came in, walked to her and stood looking down at her. There was misery in his face, a beaten look in his eyes.

"You knew I couldn't do it."

"Couldn't do what, sweet?"

"Walk out on you. I'm in love with you, goddamn it. If I stayed away tonight, I'd be back tomorrow."

Rhoda set her glass down and held out her arms. "Darling," she whispered. "You wouldn't have had to. I'd have been down in the Village after you."

He kissed her hungrily and she pressed her hand against the back of his head, holding his mouth tight to hers. His hand slipped inside her blouse. She laid her own hand on it and held it firm.

"It's for your own good, darling, that I want you to contact this Taber and demand what you're entitled to. You have a right to know. If you don't find out, there might be a policeman at your door, any minute of the day or night."

"I'll call him."

"And if he tells you it's none of your business, stand up to him."

"I will."

She allowed his hand to go on with its exploring now. His finger touched her nipple, played with it. She closed her eyes as his mouth again sought hers. "Darling . . ." she murmured.

But she was speaking to a man who had come from nowhere and had identified himself only as John Dennis. She had no number at which to call him. She could only wait until he returned again, if he ever did.

She thought: Oh, God, John Dennis. Why do you turn away from me? Why did you strip me naked and look at me as though I were a statue? Will you come back again? Please come back and make love to me.

She felt Frank Corson unsnapping her brassiere. She closed her eyes and lay back and waited, and for all the effect he had on her, Frank Corson could have been a statue.

At the last moment she insisted, "Remember, Frank, you've got to find out *everything*!"

9

The man had sallow skin; the look of a consumptive. He sat in a chair beside Crane's desk and dropped the ash from his cigar on Crane's wall-to-wall carpeting. Crane scowled, but let it pass.

"All right. Dorfman, what have you got to show for the money I've paid you?"

Dorfman, an old hand at confidential snooping, refused to quail before the much-publicized senatorial scowl. "It's tough putting on a hunt when you're not quite sure what you're after."

"I told you what I wanted. I wanted you to watch for any New York contacts Brent Taber might be using at the present time. That's simple enough, isn't it?"

"Taber contacts a lot of people. And he's a dangerous man to tail. He knows all the tricks."

"Are you telling me he caught you following him? If he did, you're no longer of any value to me."

"He didn't spot me," Dorfman said. "I followed him to New York and kept tabs on a Manhattan office, one he uses as his headquarters there."

"A directory check would tell me that."

"Take it easy. I staked out the place all day yesterday. Five men entered and left. Four were his own men."

Crane made a notation on a pad. He knew about those men. They'd been pulled off Taber's staff without notice. No doubt they'd made their last report to Taber and had headed back to Washington for reassignment. Dorfman would not know this, of course.

Or so Crane thought. Dorfman smiled as though he'd read Crane's mind and said, "I think Taber's losing his staff. They were government men—four of them—reporting in or out. My guess was *out*." He peered keenly at Crane for a moment. "Who's slicing away at Taber behind his back?"

"That's none of your—look here, Dorfman, I can get a better man than you at half the price!"

"No, you can't," Dorfman said easily. "Like I told you, there were five. The other one turned out to be a Doctor Frank Corson, an intern at Park Hill Hospital in Manhattan."

Crane made another quick notation. A Manhattan doctor. One of the androids had been found in the East River with its throat slit and a broken leg. Now a doctor had contacted Taber.

Was there a connection? Somehow, Crane had to get on the track of the tenth android Taber was hunting. Cutting the ground out from under Taber had been a satisfying victory but it wasn't enough. To be of service to his electorate, Senator Crane realized, he had to have something tangible in the way of evidence. The only way to get this was to ferret out Taber's contacts and locate the tenth android himself, or at least be there when Taber located the creature.

A man of supreme confidence in his destiny, Crane had been working on the speech he would make when he was ready for the *I accuse* scene from the Senate floor. He had even gone so far as to alert a fashionable Washington hotel to be ready with a suite at a moment's notice. Crane felt his office would be far too small to handle the traffic that would result from his revelation.

It did not occur to Crane to compliment Dorfman on his skill as an operative, for getting the book so completely and swiftly on a casual visitor to Taber's office. He said, "You've got this doctor's address?"

Dorfman put a folded slip of paper on the desk. "Another little item I'll throw in as a bonus. Taber had another tail—here in Washington."

This disturbed Crane. Did he have competition in the matter of the android? Was someone else trying to get into the act?

"A New York free-lance photographer named King. I didn't have to check on him. I recognized him. He's been around Manhattan for years."

"A photographer. What do you suppose he's up to?"

"No way of telling, at the moment. Want me to switch to him?"

"No. Stay on Taber. There's more chance there."

Dorfman got up from his chair, stepping on the ashes as he did so and ground them into the rug. "Okay, I'll report tomorrow."

After Dorfman left, Crane pondered the situation. Were the Russians behind this? Somehow, he was beginning to doubt it. And this dismayed him somewhat. He was enough of a realist to know that even a possible invasion from outer space—if that talk hadn't been a cover-up—would not carry the power of a Russian plot.

A space invasion? Too science-fictional. It had been done by H. G. Wells and God knew how many other writers. Break a yarn like that and nobody would believe it. Still, if he could get his hands on the evidence.

He scowled as he contemplated the one stone wall he hadn't been able to penetrate. No connection he had, no contact, would reveal the secret laboratory where the dissection of the androids had taken place, or the specialist who'd done the job. Porter might give it to him in exchange for a guarantee of the hydroelectric post. But Crane suspected that even Porter did not have this information. The higher you went in these top-secret projects, the more silence and stubbornness you found. The men up above, it seemed, were never as open to discussion as were the lower-echelon eager beavers. They indulged in horse-trading and played politics to a certain extent, but the lines of demarcation were sharper. That was why he could get Taber discredited, even crippled. But knocking a man of his proven ability completely out was another matter. The men on the top floor measured a lot of evidence before they acted.

But the body of one of the androids—there should be a way—there had to be a way.

Suddenly Crane smiled. Then he chuckled. Then he took an address book out of his desk drawer and thumbed through the pages.

*****

Frank Corson stared dejectedly at the carpet in Rhoda Kane's apartment. "I tried," he said. "I tried damned hard. But it just didn't do any good."

Rhoda sat beautifully poised, a picture of sophisticated perfection. She wore an obviously expensive costume featured by lounging slacks that could have been molded to her body. The afternoon sun glinted on a hairdo right out of *Vogue* or *Harper's Bazaar.* Her expression was distant; a look of impersonal pity showed on her face as she regarded Frank.

"Tell me about it, sweetie."

Frank cringed inwardly at the appellation. In Manhattan, everyone called everyone else *sweetie.*

"There wasn't much to it. I called Taber and then went down to see him. I told him exactly how I felt about things and demanded more information."

Rhoda frowned. "You *demanded*? Frank! I'm disappointed in you. The indignant citizen bit, I suppose. Don't you know how to talk to people? Your bedside manner must be tremendous."

"Rhoda! For God's sake!"

She brushed his anger away with a graceful, deprecating wave of her hand. "What did you say to him?"

"I was just telling you. I said that with a man killed in my room I had a right to some protection. I—"

"Protection! What did you do? Ask the man to hide you? Why didn't you get down on your knees and beg his pardon for living?"

Frustrated anger made Corson's lips tremble. "I did the best I could! I told him that if I couldn't find out from him what was going on, I'd go to the New York police. I told him I had a right to know about these androids."

"And he told you the only right you had was to drop dead, I suppose."

Frank Corson got to his feet. His face was stiff. His eyes were tortured. He ran a helpless hand along his jaw.

"All right, Rhoda. All right. If this is the way you want it, there's nothing I can do."

"What do you mean—the way I want it? All I've been trying to do is put a little courage into you? Didn't Taber tell you a thing about the androids?"

"He wasn't as brutal as I made it sound. In fact, he's a rather nice guy in a tough spot."

"I'm sure of that, but we couldn't care less. What did he say about the androids?"

A new, desperate wariness had been born in Frank Corson. He could take only so much and now he regarded Rhoda with a hostility of his own. "A short time ago you hooted the android idea. What changed you?"

"I use it as a term of identification! Good heavens! You act like a child. All I'm trying to do is get a little information—"

"For whom, Rhoda?"

He threw the question so suddenly it put Rhoda off balance. Quick fear flashed into her eyes. Then it vanished behind a wall of defiance.

"Are you out of your mind? Why would I have any interest in this mess except by way of protecting your interests?"

"*My* interests. I can remember not long ago when you'd have called them *our* interests."

"There you go again. Talking like a child!"

Frank crossed the room and stood close to Rhoda's chair. He looked down at her, and when he spoke there was a change in his manner. Now there was a finality in his tone that had ice in it.

"I don't know what this is all about, Rhoda, but I'm not as much of a child as you seem to think. Subjectiveness does make a person sound and act that way at times. This is a reflection of inner confusion and bewilderment. I'll admit I'm confused and bewildered. But I'm getting your message, too. I think you're telling me that whatever has happened to you is none of my business. Very well. You know where to find me if you need me."

He was walking toward the door, his back turned, so he did not see the mute appeal in Rhoda's face. "Frank—!"

He had opened the door and turned. "I'm sorry, Rhoda. I thought we had something. I'll admit I didn't handle it very well but I did my best."

He went out and closed the door softly behind him and was gone.

Pure tragedy ripped across Rhoda's eyes as she sprang to her feet, took several steps toward the door, and stopped. A wordless cry rose within her and came out as a miserable little kitten whimper.

But then she stiffened. The moment of panic passed. She straightened and touched a displaced lock of hair. The warmth of the new excitement she lived with gushed anew, and the bright, nervous smile touched her lips.

She went over, made herself a drink and went to the window. She looked down. He was out there somewhere, going about his mysterious business. The smile she thought of as soft and tender was really brittle and quite hard. She downed her drink thirstily as though it helped quench the fever in her throat.

She put the glass down and heard a whisper: "John, John, why don't you come to me? I'll help you. I'll understand. I'll teach you to make love. Let me help you, darling."

The whisper was her own and it ended in a sob.

*****

Brent Taber was studying some reports on his desk. They were not sources of satisfaction in any sense. Most of them were memos noting changes in the departmental assignments of staff men: *Due to unforeseen emergencies and the reassessment of current workloads it has become necessary to transfer from your subdepartment three . . . two . . . four . . .*

And so it went.

He sat back and closed his eyes. He was tired and he conceded it, which was a stark admission for Brent Taber. And he wondered:

Was it worth it? Banging your head against a stone wall. It would be so easy to say, *Okay, it's your world, too. If you aren't worried why should I bother?* Maybe it's not worth it. Why not assume that if there is a superior race standing off somewhere in space, they're only a bunch of paper tigers and to hell with it. Or maybe they wish us only the best. Maybe—

The door opened. Marcia Holly pushed her head in. "Have you eaten anything today?"

"Get lost, sweetheart," Brent said absently.

"Maybe you look on eating as a bad habit, like sleeping, but it would be nice to avoid a breakdown and stay out of the hospital, too."

"You're such a pleasant person to have around, except when you get up off your chair and start making noises like a woman."

"Just to accommodate you, I'll change my sex. But right now, there's a man to see you."

"Tell him to go to hell but don't offend him."

"I think you ought to see him. He's got an official paper of some kind. You didn't steal a car or anything, did you?"

"I parked in the middle of an intersection, but I didn't think they'd mind." Brent Taber sighed. "All right. Send him in."

The man was small, ingrown and, as Brent Taber learned, somewhat stubborn.

"My name is Charles Blackwell," he said. "My brother has been lost for over two months now."

"I'm sorry," Brent said politely.

"My brother was a source of concern to us—"

"Who is *us?*"

"Why, the family. Who else? We all worried about Charlie. He had fits of depression. Kind of a maniac-depressive."

"*Manic*-depressive," Taber corrected gently.

"Yeah, that kind, ah—kind of. Well anyhow, he hides from us sometimes and we worry."

"Who sent you to me?"

Charles Blackwell waved a vague hand, "Oh, they told me you were the man to see."

"Tell me their names," Brent said politely. "I'd like to thank them personally."

"Oh that won't be necessary—not necessary at all. You see the thing is, my brother Jack has accidents sometimes and so we figured he might have broken a leg or something, maybe, and it seems you—well, you kind of turned out to be the man to see about it." Charles Blackwell waved the paper. "With this."

Good lord, Taber groaned inwardly. This thing is turning into a comic opera—plain slapstick.

"And why am I the man to see?"

"Because they said you knew about a man with a broken leg who got killed or something."

"They said that?"

"Uh-huh, and if you'd just let me see the man, I could tell in a jiffy whether he's Jack or not."

It had been a pretty long speech and Charles Blackwell seemed happy to get it off his chest. He felt he'd earned a cigarette so he lit one.

Brent Taber watched the match go out and then said, "You're the Goddamnedest phony I've met this week."

"They said you'd say that, but all I want is to see the man and then I'll know. I'll tell you in a jiffy if he's my brother."

"All right."

Charles Blackwell gulped a throatful of smoke in disbelief. Evidently they'd told him it wouldn't be as easy as this. They must have told him it would be as hard as hell, because he stared at Brent as though the latter hadn't played fair.

Brent reached into a drawer and took out a glossy photo. He pushed it across the desk. Charles Blackwell craned his neck, looked, and saw what appeared to be a man lying naked on a marble slab with his throat cut.

Blackwell swallowed hard and nodded and said, "Yeah, that's Jack, all right."

"How do you know?"

"I can tell."

"You can?"

Charles Blackwell got a little indignant. "Of course, I can. Don't you think a man knows his own brother?"

"That depends on which man and what brother."

"I want the body of my relative," Charles Blackwell said.

"I'll see you in hell first," Brent Taber replied pleasantly. "Now get out of my office before I send for the man who uses the broom around here."

Charles Blackwell was more comfortable now—more confident. "That's what they told me you'd say, so they gave me this to bring. It's a court order signed by a judge who sits in a court and listens to people's beefs about getting pushed around and does something about it."

Brent Taber took the paper and peered at the signature. "It figures," he said softly. "It figures right down the line."

"He's a fine judge," Charles Blackwell said virtuously.

"He's a skunk. He'll sign anything there's a buck in, and sometimes he'll do it for fifty cents. He'd be a disgrace even to a park bench, and why they haven't caught up with him I'll never know."

"A fine man," Charles Blackwell said, "and the paper is as legal as—"

"Oh, it's legal all right."

Brent Taber lapsed into silence and Charles Blackwell seemed happy to allow him this privilege. All I need, Brent thought, is a court-defiance rap charged against me. Is that what Crane is trying to get? Did he expect me to throw this creep out of my office and leave myself wide open? Maybe, maybe not. If not, what is Crane after? He's certainly achieved his purpose in getting even with an upstart government appointee.

"Okay," Brent Taber said decisively. "You can have the body. Come with me."

He got up, put on his hat, and strode out through the reception room and into the corridor. Charles Blackwell came scuttling along behind. Brent ignored the elevators and went through a door marked *Stairway* and started down at a fast clip. Charles Blackwell came clopping along behind.

Six flights lower down, Blackwell gasped, "Why don't we use the el—elevator?"

Brent ignored him and went down seventeen more flights. Charles Blackwell was livid when they reached the bottom.

"For Christ sake—!"

Taber walked to the curb and dived out into traffic. Blackwell plunged out after him, horns snarling and general indignation ruling above the chaos.

They reached the opposite curb through some obscure miracle, with Blackwell hanging on grimly until Taber pushed a door open and plunged into a thick odor of formaldehyde.

"Have you still got that court order?" Taber asked as though hopeful of a negative answer.

Blackwell held it up triumphantly. A few minutes later, he was gaping down at a hasty reassembly of what had once been the ninth android.

He swallowed hard and said, "Nope. It ain't Jack."

"You're sure?" Taber said sarcastically. "It looks just like the picture.

"Not quite. Anyhow, it ain't Jack."

The mystified Dr. Entman eyed Taber quizzically. "What's this all about?"

Taber jerked a thumb in the direction of Blackwell. "The eleventh android," he said tersely, and strode out of the laboratory.

Dr. Entman shook his head sadly, certain that Taber had slipped a cog.

*****

Charles Blackwell, a trifle ill from the smell of formaldehyde, stood on the corner, closed his eyes, and took a deep breath. When he opened his eyes a man in a blue suit was standing beside him.

"I would like you to answer some questions for me," the man said.

Blackwell gulped and blinked. "Sorry, mister, I'm kind of a stranger here myself."

"That man you entered this building with—what business did you have with him?"

It should have occurred to Charles Blackwell that this was none of the stranger's business, but it didn't. That thought came later but, at the moment, as he looked into the man's oddly empty eyes, his question seemed entirely justified.

"Well, you see, my brother Jack bothers us, kind of. He gets manic-depressive spells."

"What did that have to do with Brent Taber?"

"We thought maybe my brother broke his leg and then dropped dead or—or something. Anyhow, I got this here court order—they gave it to me—and I showed it to Taber—"

"Who are *they*?"

Blackwell felt strangely excited. He felt as though this man were a friend, although he didn't know quite why.

"Well, you see I've been around a long time. I run errands and things for Senator Crane. I'm confidential to him, you understand, because I never talk. I always keep my mouth shut. So he trusts me and he gave me this here court order—"

"Who is Senator Crane?"

"You don't know Senator Crane? You new in this country

maybe?"

"He is a government official?"

"He's elected to office. He's a United States Senator. Anyhow, Brent Taber showed me this here guy all cut up and I said it wasn't Jack and—well, that was that."

"What room did Brent Taber take you to?"

"The damn place smelled like a skunk factory."

"What room number?"

"Ten twenty-six—I think. Yeah, ten twenty-six it was, and I'm telling you, if you go in there, for Christ sake wear a gas mask. I damn near—"

But Charles Blackwell was talking to himself. The man had turned away abruptly and was now disappearing around the corner.

"I wonder what the hell he wanted?" Blackwell asked plaintively. Then he hailed a cab and went to report to Senator Crane.

*****

The tenth android stood with his back to the window in Les King's room in Manhattan and said, "There is something I want you to do. If you are very careful, you will succeed. If you succeed, there is a great deal of money in it for you."

The fear that grew in Les King when they were apart, the uneasy feeling that maybe money wasn't the most important thing in the world, died automatically as John Dennis stared at him through those strangely empty eyes.

"Is it something I can handle?"

"Yes." Dennis handed King a folded slip of paper. "I have written down an address there. It is in Washington, D.C. I want you to enter those premises—that room—and find some reports that should be there."

"Reports on what?"

"It is a dissecting place of some kind. That's where the bodies of the androids are. The man who is doing it must have reports. There must be records that tell what was wrong with the androids. It must be put down somewhere why they died."

"Does it matter?"

"It is a matter of vital importance. There will be much money for you if you get those reports and give them to me."

"Who pays the money?"

"I will pay it to you if you get the reports."

The prospect was exciting to King. Later, there could be a

story about how he got vital pictures of the project. His thinking had changed, but this did not seem odd to him. All thought of functioning in counterespionage against the Russians had moved into the back of his mind. He was in the game now for the money. Oh was it that? Maybe he was in it for the excitement. There was something in the man who called himself John Dennis that generated excitement. It was like living a melodrama. It tingled in the blood and took a man out of the drab world where every day was like the one before it.

"I'll try," Les King said.

"You will succeed."

"I will succeed."

Jesus! This man had a thing about him. He inspired you. When he looked at you with those weird eyes, you just knew you couldn't fail.

10

The doorbell rang. Rhoda Kane sprang up from the sofa and almost spilled her drink. She was halfway across the room before she realized she was almost running. She stopped. The hand that held the cocktail glass shook.

Resolutely, she steadied, crossed to the liquor cabinet, put down the glass, and went calmly to the door.

He stood there looking at her through those oddly empty eyes which, through some contradiction of all probability, warmed her.

He came in and closed the door, saying nothing. A touch of panic rippled through her. He was so silent, so unbending, so impersonal. Was this a reflection of her inability to communicate with him? Could their relationship fail because of this short-coming on her part? What good was love if you couldn't communicate it to the loved one?

She moved into his arms and raised her lips. His arms went around her, but there was no pressure or affection in them. Their lips were an inch apart. Her urge was to give full rein to the heady happiness and excitement within her—to show her love in a kiss.

But she held off and, after a few moments, he drew, back, raised one hand and passed it through her hair. Not with affection, she thought, but rather with curiosity; almost as though he were preoccupied with its composition. He rolled a strand of hair between thumb and finger, testing it.

"It needs cutting," Rhoda said.

"Do you cut it?"

She laughed nervously. "You don't know much about women, do you."

"I know nothing about woman."

Trying to inject a gay note into her voice, she said, "We eat, we sleep, we—we're very functional, really."

He rubbed a finger down her cheek. He pressed the flesh on her neck and watched the muscle spring back as he withdrew his finger.

"Do that to me," he said.

Mystified, Rhoda pressed her finger against his neck until she could feel a pulse in his throat. She withdrew the finger. "Like that?"

"Did it leave a mark?"

"No. Is there something wrong? Do you have a sore throat?"

"My throat is not sore."

Rhoda's frustration was a pitiful thing. How could she get to him? How could she break through his shyness?

"I think you're afraid of me," she said lightly.

He did not answer. He took a backward step and regarded her for a moment with a frown. Then he began to unbutton her blouse.

Rhoda wanted to object. An instinctive protest caused her to draw back. His only reaction to this was to step forward and continue to unbutton her blouse. She wanted to resist but the fear of driving him away held her mute; that and something in his eyes that told of excitement, an unformed phantom of delight that had never materialized but still held sway over her through promise.

He stripped the blouse off. She wore no brassiere underneath, and he regarded her breasts somberly. He pressed a nipple with the tip of one finger and watched it spring back into place.

"Please. I—"

He ignored her. He pressed the nipple again and then found the zipper on the side of her slacks. He pulled it down and pushed the slacks down over her hips. She lifted each foot obediently.

He was on his knees now, running his fingers gently down her thighs. Rhoda trembled at the touch. Then she realized it was not love-making on his part—not in any sense. He was preoccupied with the fine hair on her skin. He studied it closely.

"I should have shaved my legs," Rhoda said uncertainly. He raised his head, the cold eyes trained into hers. "This hair grows, too?"

Rhoda caught her lower lip between her teeth. Tears were close to the surface.

This is crazy. This is utterly insane. I'm mad or he's mad. I don't know. I just don't know . . .

The last garment was removed and she was naked there in the middle of the living room. He studied her body again, that passionless, preoccupied frown on his face. He drew her down onto the floor and, for a moment, the room spun around Rhoda, her emotional entrapment now the focal point, the eye of the storm that raged in her being. He went on with his minute inspection of her person.

No—no. Please don't. Please don't treat me like this. I'm a woman. Don't be contemptuous of me. Oh, no—please. Don't degrade and humiliate me like this.

There was sudden pain. Rhoda's body wrenched and heaved upward. With a sob, she sank back to the floor.

I must fight. I must not allow this. I must not let him do these cruel, degrading things to me. I must fight but I am afraid to. I am afraid he'll go away and never come back—and if he did that, there would be nothing left for me.

John Dennis seemed to become aware for the first time that certain manipulations caused reaction—the jerking of Rhoda's body and her involuntary cry of pain. He repeated the manipulation with his eyes on her face.

I cannot allow this. I must fight. I must resist. Oh, Rhoda Kane, what has happened to you? Frank, please help, help me. Frank—

But something seemed to flow out of John Dennis and into her mind and soul and spirit; something that made the flesh and what was done to the flesh unimportant.

The touch of John Dennis' hand brought fright as it foretold further pain and degradation. Rhoda sobbed inwardly and braced herself to withstand whatever was to come.

Mad!—mad!—mad!

But it meant nothing.

*****

The building was not for tourists. It wasn't like the Pentagon or the White House or any of the other historical or glamour symbols in Washington, D.C. It was on a side street, and while no one associated it with governmental activity, it was of a size and importance that justified a uniformed attendant in the lobby.

He was a hard-bitten old Irishman named Callahan, and nobody got past him without justification. Also, he was a man of robust hates and great loyalties; a man whom Brent Taber was honored to call friend.

He was also a man Brent Taber was waiting to hear from.

The call came late in the afternoon of the day following Charles Blackwell's search for his would-be brother. Taber picked up the phone.

"It's me—Callahan. He's here, Mr. Taber."

"Thanks. I'll be right over."

"And be hurrying right along if you want to get here in time. He's not one to be restrained indefinitely."

"Tell him the elevator's busted."

Brent Taber slammed the phone down and left. He used an

elevator this time and went across town in a cab. Even then, he was almost too late. As he arrived at his destination, Senator Crane was protesting loudly.

"It's just plain stupidity. Elevators don't quit running for no reason. Find a burnt-out fuse. Do something! And do it quick or I'll phone somebody who will!"

"Well, I'll be blessed," Callahan said, completely crest-fallen. "It was the switch, Senator. The blessed switch was off."

"Well, turn it on and get me up to ten."

"Good afternoon, Senator."

Crane whirled. "Brent Taber!" He threw a quick scowl at Callahan and was on the verge of accusing the Irishman of high treason, but he said, "All right. I'm glad you're here, Taber. We might as well get this thing into the open. Are you going to take me to room ten twenty-six or do I have to take steps to force your co-operation?"

Taber stared morosely at Crane's nose. "Why, Senator, where did you get the idea my department wouldn't help a member of Congress to the utmost?"

"None of your sarcasm. Let's go upstairs."

"All right, Callahan. Let's go upstairs."

They got off on ten and walked down the corridor. "Ten twenty-eight, you said?"

"You know damned well what I said."

Taber opened the door. He stood aside. Crane walked in and stopped dead. He again whirled on Crane.

"It's empty."

"That's right. I could have told you downstairs but you wouldn't have believed me. What were you looking for? New quarters?"

"Taber, I'll break you for this! If you think you can thwart the will of the United States Senate—"

"You've been doing a pretty good job of breaking already."

"I haven't even begun!"

"That still doesn't tell me what you thought you'd find."

"Quit being cute. This time yesterday there were cadavers in here. This was a laboratory!"

Brent looked wearily at his watch. "You're wrong, Senator. This place was vacated exactly an hour and fifteen minutes after your stooge used his court order to locate the cadavers."

"Then you admit you defied a court order—"

"Oh, come off of it. The court order said nothing about leaving things as they were. But that's not important. The important thing is that you give me some understanding and sympathy."

This obviously astounded Crane. "From you? That from the cocky, self-sufficient Brent Taber? That's a little different tune from the one you sang in your office, not too long ago."

"All right. I'll concede that. Let's say you've got me licked. I'll admit I should have reacted a little less arrogantly. My nerves were shot. I'd been up late too often. Now I'm ready to be reasonable."

Crane was scowling. "This isn't like you, Taber—not like you at all. I'm suspicious. Why are you suddenly so agreeable?"

"Because I believe the nation—the world—is in great danger. I think we should all realize that danger and work together."

"Then why have you been fighting me?"

"Because I honestly felt it was the best thing to do. I've changed my mind. I'm willing to tell you the whole story."

"I've heard the whole story. I—"

"Then it was you who had my office taped."

"Exactly. I'm not ashamed of it. When I'm fighting for my constituents I use every weapon at my command."

Brent Taber regarded Crane narrowly. "I underestimated your abilities, Senator. That was fast work. Twenty minutes after I refused you permission to attend that meeting, you had your man briefed and in action. It was the waiter who brought in the coffee, wasn't it?"

Before Crane could answer, Taber gestured and said, "Never mind. That's not important. You've heard the tape, so tell me—what do you want from me? How can I earn your co-operation?"

"Quite simply, Taber. By recognizing my authority as a United States Senator. By keeping me briefed on your progress against this terrible thing that menaces our people. By accepting my active co-operation in destroying it."

"What exactly do you mean by *active*?"

"Just what the word implies. Have the men on the senatorial committee you briefed been at all active in helping you?"

"Frankly, no."

"Then what right have they to expect any rewards—shall we say?—for their efforts?"

"You may have a point."

"I believe in rewards where rewards are due."

"And you want—?"

"In plain terms, the right to association in the public mind with the effort to protect the nation."

"You want favorable publicity if and when this matter makes headlines?"

"Is that too much to ask?"

Brent Taber suddenly seemed lost and, in truth, he was wondering why in hell he'd approached Crane in this way. He felt ashamed for even considering the possibility of bending to the will of a windbag like Crane. *Good Lord*, he thought, *I must be tired. I was on the point of playing the jellyfish.*

Abruptly his voice sharpened. "I'm sorry, I can't promise you that."

"Taber, you're a fool! I'll get it anyhow. I told you I'd break you if you got in my way, and you've been almost discredited already. Don't you know when to quit?"

"Maybe that's my trouble, Senator. Maybe I'm bull-headed. Anyhow, right or wrong, I'll play out this string to the end. Good day—and I hope you enjoy your new offices."

*****

An hour later, back at his own phone, Taber got a second call from Callahan. "There's another one."

"Another one? I don't follow you."

"A photographer from New York City. He's being real cagey, this one, but I know the breed. The kind that's so stupid-clever he outsmarts himself."

"What's he after?"

"Sounds to me like he wants the same thing as the Senator."

"Hmmm," Taber mused. "Those are mighty popular cadavers, aren't they, Callahan?"

"I'm blessed if they aren't."

"All right. You tell Mr. King—that is his name, isn't it?"

"You've got good eyesight—reading a blasted press card from clear across town."

"I'm clairvoyant, Callahan. Tell you what you do—give me fifteen minutes to make a phone call and then send him after the bodies."

"To the right place?"

"To the right place. And hold out for a good price. Get what the traffic will bear. I'd say maybe fifty dollars. Allow yourself to be bribed real good."

"I'll do that."

11

As with Rhoda Kane's mind, Les King's seemed to be divided into two sections. One of these kept him in a state of perpetual uneasiness at what the other was forcing him to do. He realized that venting your frustrations against bureaucrats was one thing, but actively engaging in dangerous snooping was quite another.

In the moments of uncertainty after John Dennis sent him to Washington, D.C. with orders to get his hands on certain data, Les King bolstered his courage by telling himself that, what the hell, he'd planned all along to go right ahead and dig out the complete android through whatever means possible. Therefore, meeting and teaming up with Dennis had been a big break.

The rationalization wasn't too comforting, though, because he knew he could never have gone ahead on his own. Also, he realized he and Dennis weren't a team at all. Dennis ordered; he obeyed. Still, the sense of excitement Dennis generated in him had its effect on the other part of his mind, and this was the stronger; this held sway. Somehow, there was the certainty that Dennis did not make mistakes; that everything would work out.

This conviction was jarred a little when he got past the lobby man in the Washington building—a feat easily accomplished—climbed ten flights of stairs, and found room ten twenty-eight empty. Obviously, Dennis had goofed.

King's first instinct was to retreat as quietly as he'd advanced; to get away from the place and report failure to Dennis. But as he went back downstairs, the thought of Dennis' disapproval began weighing more heavily. Maybe something unforeseen had happened. Maybe he could still pull this one out of the fire.

With this hope foremost in his mind, he went into the lobby, assumed a bold front, and demanded: "Where in the hell did the people in ten twenty-eight go?"

And the front worked. The lobby man, a big Irishman, was so impressed he didn't even ask King how he'd gotten into the building. He blinked politely and said, "Blessed if I'm not new here myself. This is my first day. What room was it?"

Then the big Irishman went to a phone to check, and came back with a Georgetown address written out on a slip of paper. Georgetown seemed like an unlikely place to find cadavers and, under normal conditions, King would have been highly suspicious of the whole thing. But what the hell? Nothing was normal about this project, so why not follow through?

King, you're crazy. You're out of your stupid mind.

He raised his hand and a cab cut in toward the curb.

When he arrived at the address, he found himself standing on the walk in front of a large, imposing house. The place still seemed unlikely but you never could tell. The way things were these days, any house in whatever neighborhood was a potential location for almost anything. The way this one was laid out, there could possibly have been a laboratory in the back. A narrow walk led in that direction and, instead of climbing the front steps, King followed it around the corner and found a basement door at the foot of a flight of steps.

He hesitated before ringing the bell. What kind of an approach would he use? The idea was to get inside and see the layout—spot the office, the file cabinets. The feature-story bit? It might work, but who the hell lived here? He'd checked the mailbox beside the front porch but there'd been no name.

Deciding he could only play it by ear, he pulled in his diaphragm and rang the bell.

The door opened quickly—too quickly, it seemed—and King realized he'd struck a pay lode in the myopic-looking little jerk who stood peering out at him. The guy wore a white laboratory coat with two bloodstains on it and was holding a scalpel in his hand.

"I'm Doctor Entman. Can I help you?"

Entman—Entman—for Christ sake. Oh, sure, a neurologist. Had to be the same guy. International authority. The *Times* once did a feature on his arrival at Idlewild. UN stuff.

"I'm King of the *Herald Tribune*," Les said, lying easily. "We're shaping up a feature on the more advanced neurological techniques—Sunday supplement material. They sent me down to see if you'd give us some of your views."

"I'd be delighted. Come in. Come in."

"I'm not imposing on your time, I hope."

"Not at all!"

The guy was almost too cordial, but what the hell? All their noses twitched at the smell of publicity.

Entman led him down a cement-floored corridor, the smell of formaldehyde thickening as they went, then into a small office with an open door, on the far side through which Les King was confronted with a frankly gruesome sight—a dissecting room with parts of cadavers lying around like orders in a meat packer's shipping room.

"Won't you sit down, please? There by the desk."

As Entman gestured, he noted King's reaction to the sight and the smell of the dissecting room.

"Just a moment. I'll close that door."

"No, don't bother, Doctor. I'd better get the authentic atmosphere. It makes a better story."

"I admire your courage, young man."

King pointed toward the room. "Something important?"

"Routine—only routine."

Then, to Les King's practiced eye, Entman proved it wasn't routine at all by entering the laboratory and gathering up a loose pile of notes lying there on a table. He seemed to momentarily forget King's presence as he went through the notes, sorted them carefully, and brought them back into the office.

King watched as Entman then deposited them in a small safe. He closed the safe but didn't lock it. Then he turned, beamed myopically at his visitor, and said, "Now I'm at your service, young man."

"Fine, Doctor. Now, this series we're planning will highlight modern techniques with an eye to illustrating . . ."

While King asked questions and Entman answered, another part of King's mind was busy with the real problem at hand. Entman would, no doubt, lock the safe before he left the office. Burglary—a risk King was willing to take—would get him back into the office when no one was around, but how could he open the safe? Walking straight to the thing he was after had been fine. Having been put in a position to get to know what the notes looked like was another astounding piece of good fortune. All this, however, could turn out to mean nothing because he didn't know how to crack a safe.

He would have to report failure after being so close.

"As I said," Entman prattled on happily, "when I was at Johns Hopkins I—"

The desk phone rang. Entman picked it up, answered it and then hung up. "Would I impose if I asked you for a fifteen-minute break? Some people are calling that I must see—an appointment I forgot."

"Not at all," Les King assured him. "I'd like to do a little work on these notes to see if I left out anything."

"So good of you. Boring people, really. I'll get rid of them as soon as possible."

Entman left through an inner door and King was stunned by his good luck. He called it that even while experience and judgment shrieked warnings. This was too pat—too easy. Something was phony in the setup.

But he didn't even have to fight what common sense was telling him. He was too busy opening the safe, spreading the data out on the desktop, and using a small camera he carried in the side pocket of his jacket.

Then, he put the data back in the safe and felt the hot, excitement surge up through his body.

*****

"I'm afraid I owe you a drink," Entman said ruefully.

"You were right. When I got back to the office, he was gone."

Brent Taber grinned, but only with his mouth—his eyes remained somber and weary. "The data was back in the safe?"

"Right where I put it. I'll swear it hadn't been moved."

"He was photographing it thirty seconds after you left."

"But how can you be sure?"

Brent Taber pulled at his ear and stared at a Renoir on the wall of Entman's drawing room without seeing it. "I can't, of course. We can't be sure of anything. It's all based on an idea you gave me."

"What idea?"

"You told me the results of your research on the androids would be valuable to whoever built them—as a guide to perfecting androids that wouldn't die under earth conditions."

"That was obvious logic."

"And it ties in with another thought. A race of beings as advanced as these could take us over without trouble, it would seem."

"Quite true. Except—"

"Except that they themselves may not be able to exist on earth, either; no more so than we could exist on the moon without creating conditions favorable to our physical capabilities."

"So . . . ?"

"So I'm betting that the ten androids were sent here on a trial-and-error basis, with the objective of perfecting them and creating an android army to move in and take us over."

"It's a thought, but with their power they could achieve the same result with less effort by pulverizing us. Or so it would seem to me."

"True, but maybe they don't want us pulverized; maybe they'd rather take over a working planet than a lot of rubble."

"All that follows logically," Entman admitted, "provided the original hypothesis is true—that they cannot invade us in person."

"Right. But I've got to start somewhere and hope I'm on the right track."

"One thing occurs to me. Eight of the androids died and one was killed. What if all ten had succumbed? How did they plan to get their data?"

"Who knows? I'm not saying the idea is foolproof. But a certain amount of risk had to be involved. If the ten died, they would have missed. Maybe they'd try again in that case. But they were lucky—one survived."

Entman was peering thoughtfully at nothing. "Your idea is bolstered by the fact that the androids were found all over the country. They could have been testing various climates."

"But it's weakened by the creatures being found in cities—the least likely places to escape detection. Why didn't they stay in isolated sections?"

Entman smiled. "I like the way you reach out for arguments against your own theory, but you reached too far for that one. If they'd done that, who would find the androids and do the research work?"

Brent Taber brightened. "You comfort me, Doctor. That little thread got lost in my maze. They wanted the creatures to be found. They didn't expect to fool us. Why else would the one in Chicago go brazenly into a tavern, start to drink and then get into an argument?"

"That's right. The argument must have been started deliberately." Entman beamed on Taber. "I think we deserve another Scotch."

Entman poured the drink. He looked kindly at Taber as he handed it to him, and made what seemed an abrupt change in subject. "They're giving you a very hard time, aren't they, son?"

Taber considered the question as he downed a healthy belt from the glass. "I guess you could call it that. I'm getting pretty unpopular in some places. As a matter of fact, I've wondered why you stick by me."

Entman poured himself a drink. "That hurts me a little, son."

"I'm sorry. It's getting so I don't even know how to treat a friend."

Entman raised his glass in salute. "I'm afraid this sentimental chit-chat doesn't become either of us. Let's go back to our friend from the *Herald Tribune*. You're sure he photographed the data?"

"I think we can depend on it."

"When I got your call, I acted as fast as I could. The data looks authentic, I'm sure, but it was a quick job of fiction. Now I'd like to know the rest—whatever you didn't have time to tell me."

"It's still a logic-chain, with some pretty flimsy strands in some places, but I'm afraid I'm stuck with it. King was greedy and hungry when I first talked to him, but I think I scared him off. I think, left to himself, he would have let the thing alone.

"So I was surprised when he showed up at the old location. My first thought was that Crane had sent him. It would have been logical—Crane sending a man to try and find out where we'd taken the cadavers he obviously wants to get his hands on.

"But I couldn't connect Crane with King. I couldn't figure how Crane could have known of King's existence." Taber paused to drink and grin his humorless grin. "So I made a daring leap. If it had to be someone else, why not the tenth android himself?"

Entman frowned as he toyed with the idea. "Why, good lord—!"

"You said yourself that the androids probably possessed extraordinary powers."

"Yes, but—"

"All right. If we accept the need-of-data theory, which we have to, what would the tenth android be doing? Trying to get his hands on it. He could conceivably have made contact with King. King took a picture of the ninth android. Our still able and functioning number ten found his way to Doctor Corson's room in Greenwich Village and demolished number nine, for reasons of his own, so he could have made contact with King, put him under domination, and sent him after the data."

"How could he know where the data was?"

Taber shrugged. "I said there were some pretty weak strings in my logic. But it so shaped, as I saw it, where it would stand or smash on one point. If King had waited in your office for your return, I would have been forced to assume he was there on his own. But he left, so I'm going to figure he took what he came for—the bait you dangled under his nose."

"That brings up a question in my mind. If you're right, King will now make contact with the android, will he not?"

"I assume he will."

"And that will give you a chance to capture him and have the whole ten accounted for?"

"I don't want him until he sends the data back to whoever is waiting for it."

"You'd like to have them build their synthetic army on the specifications I made out?"

"I'd dearly love that."

"Do you know where to contact King again?"

"He's being tailed. They stripped me, but I still have two men left."

"You're being treated miserably!" Entman scowled. "I'm going to talk to some people about this. I refuse to allow—"

"Thanks, but not for a while. I've shaped my operation on a one-man basis. I'd be embarrassed if they relented. I wouldn't know what to do with all the men."

Entman's little eyes shone with affection. "I can only wish you good luck."

"Thanks. I'll need it."

"And one more thing I was wondering."

"What's that?"

"Why do you suppose the tenth android killed the one in the Village?"

"Another case of taking one reason for want of a better one. I think it was his way of delivering the creature to us for research. He couldn't know for sure that we already had his 'brothers.'"

"You're right—you must be," Entman agreed.

"Small consolation. I'd like a few facts to go on for a change instead of having to depend on logic all the time," Taber growled.

"What are you referring to?"

"The data. I'm assuming, *if* that's what's important, that the tenth creature has a way of getting the stuff back up there."

"I can help a little on that," Entman said. "I can assure you that from what I've found in those brains, the data could, most likely, be sent mentally."

"You're sure of that?"

"I've found a certain part of those brains developed in a peculiar way—"

Taber smiled. "You're sure of that?"

"Well . . . that's my theory. It would appear logical that—"

Taber leaned forward suddenly and extended his glass, the grin on his face showing some genuine humor. "Let's have another drink, Doctor. Then I'll go. I love the factual way this Scotch of yours hits my stomach."

12

Frank Corson entered the office of Wilson Maynard, Superintendent of Park Hill Hospital. Maynard looked out over the tops of his old-fashioned pince-nez glasses and said, "Oh, Doctor Corson. You phoned for a chat."

It was the rather pompous superintendent's way of saying he was happy to give Frank Corson a little time. He considered all the doctors and nurses at Park Hill his "boys and girls," and he did the "father" bit very well.

"Yes, I—"

Maynard peered even harder. "You don't look well, Frank. Pale. You've been working too hard."

"Nothing important, Doctor Maynard."

"Sit down. Will you have a cigarette?"

"No, thank you. I just wanted to ask you about a transfer."

"A transfer!" This was amazing. "Aren't you happy at Park Hill?"

"I've been very happy."

Maynard went swiftly through a card file on his desk. "You have—let's see—five more months of internship. Then—"

"Then I'd planned to enter private practice. But something personal has come up and I think a change is for the best."

"I'm certainly sorry to hear that."

"One of the men I graduated with went to a hospital in a small Minnesota town. We've corresponded and he's given me a pretty clear picture—a nice town, a need for doctors and physicians—"

"But we need them here in the East, too."

"I realize that, and I'm making the move with some regret. But, frankly, New York City no longer appeals to me. I think perhaps a small hospital is more suited to my temperament."

"I'm certainly sorry to hear this, Corson. But I won't try to dissuade you. Normally, I might bring a little more personal pressure to bear, but I sense that your mind is made up. We're sorry to see you go, but the best of luck to you."

"Thank you, sir."

After Frank Corson left, Superintendent Maynard sorted a memo out of the pile on his desk. The memo concerned Frank Corson. Superintendent Maynard reread it and thought how well things usually worked out. Now it wouldn't be necessary to have that talk with Corson about sloppy work. Obviously there had been something on the young intern's mind for weeks now. Too bad. But let the Minnesota hospital, wherever it was, worry about the trouble and perhaps put Corson on the right track again.

He was their baby now.

Maynard took Corson's card from the files and wrote across it: *Transfer approved with regret.*

*****

Brent Taber stood in the shelter of a doorway on the Lower East Side of Manhattan and watched an entrance across the street. He had been there for over an hour.

Another hour passed and Taber shifted from one aching foot to the other as a man in a blue suit emerged from the entrance and moved off down the street.

When the man had turned a corner, Taber crossed over and looked up at the brownstone. It was a perfect place to hide—one of the many rooming houses in the city where, if you paid your rent and kept your peace, no one cared who you were or where you came from.

Not even, Taber reflected, if you had been born in a laboratory and had come from someplace among the stars.

He climbed the steps of the brownstone and tried the knob. The door opened. He went inside and found himself in a drab, dark hall furnished with an umbrella stand, a worn carpet, and a table spread with mail.

There was a bell on the table. He tapped it and, after a lazy length of time, a shapeless woman came through a door on the right and regarded him with no great show of cordiality.

"Nothing vacant, mister. Everything I've got is rented."

"I wasn't looking for a room. I'm just doing a little checking."

"My license is okay," the woman said belligerently. "The place is clean and orderly."

"That's not what I'm checking about. There's been some counterfeit money passed in this neighborhood and we're trying to trace it down."

The woman had a pronounced mustache that quivered at this news. "Counterfeit! My roomers are honest."

"I'm sure they are. But some people carry counterfeit money without knowing it. Do they all pay in cash?"

"Only two of them."

"Men or women?"

"One girl—Katy Wynn."

"Where does she work?"

"Down in Wall Street."

"Not much chance we're interested. This money has been turning up around Times Square."

"The other's a man—quiet, no trouble, pays his rent right on the dot every week. John Dennis his name is and he doesn't look like no counterfeiter."

Taber took a forward step. "What's his room number?"

"Six—on the second floor. But he isn't in now. He just went out."

"Okay. Maybe I'll be back. As I said, we don't suspect anybody. We're just checking for sources."

Taber turned toward the door. The woman vanished back into her own quarters as Taber snapped the lock. He stood in the vestibule for a minute or two, studying some cards he took from his pocket, and when she did not reappear, he opened the door, went back in, and climbed the stairs.

The door to number six was not locked. Taber went inside. The window was small and gave on an areaway. He could see nothing until he turned on the light. Even then, he could see nothing of interest—the room was ordinary in every sense.

But as Brent Taber checked it out, some unusual aspects became apparent. There were two pieces of luggage in the closet. One, an oversized suitcase, stood on end.

And jammed neatly down behind it was the body of Les King. His throat had been cut.

Brent Taber stared down into the closet for what seemed like an interminable time. His eyes were bleak and his mouth was grim and stiff as he passed a slow hand along his jaw.

He took a long, backward step and closed his eyes for a moment as though hoping the whole improbable mess would go away. But it was still there when he opened them again.

He turned, went downstairs, and took the receiver off the phone on the wall by the front door.

The shapeless landlady came out again. She scowled at Taber. "What are you doing here?"

He regarded her with a kind of affectionate weariness. "Have you got a dime, lady?"

Gaping, she pawed into her apron pocket and handed him a coin.

"Thanks much." He dialed. "Is Captain Abrams there?"

There was a wait, during which Brent Taber asked the oddly bemused landlady: "Are you afraid of the dead?"

But before she could decide whether she was or not, Taber turned to the phone. "Captain? . . . That's right, Brent Taber . . . No, right, here in Manhattan. There's been a little trouble. You'd better come over personally."

He turned to the landlady. "What's the address here, sister?"

And later, with the landlady back in her lair, Brent Taber sat down on the stairs to wait; sat there with surprise at the feeling of relief that filled his mind. He had no feeling of triumph about it; no sense of a job well done. But there was no great guilt at having failed, either.

Mostly, he thought, it was the simplification that had come about. There had been so many confusing and bewildering complications in the affair; improbability piled on the impossible; the ridiculous coupled with the incredible.

But now, with one stroke of a knife, it had been simplified and brought into terms everyone could understand; into terms Captain Abrams of the New York Police Department would grasp in an instant.

A killer was on the loose.

*****

One of Senator Crane's priceless gifts was a sense of timing. Much of his success had sprung from the instinctive knowledge of when to act. He had a sense of the dramatic which never deserted him. As a result, he had been known to turn in an instant from one subject to another—to dodge defeats and score triumphs with bewildering agility.

His preoccupation on this particular day was with a home-state issue—the location of a government plant. After he obtained the floor, he counted the house and noted that only a bare quorum was present. Gradually, the members of the Senate of the United States would drift to their seats. So Crane began reading letters which tended to support his state's claim to the new plant and the benefits that would accrue therefrom.

Crane droned on. The Vice-President of the United States looked down on the top of Senator Crane's massive head and became fruitfully preoccupied with thoughts of his own.

Then, quite suddenly, the line of Crane's exposition changed. The Vice-President wasn't quite sure at what precise point this had come about. He wasn't aware of the change until some very strange words penetrated:

". . . so, therefore, it has become starkly apparent that the American people have been denied the information which would have made them aware of their own deadly danger. Invasion from space is now imminent."

The Vice-President tensed. Had the stupid idiot gone mad? Or had he, the Vice-President, been in a fog when vital, top-secret information had been made public?

He banged the gavel down hard, for want of a better gesture, and was grateful when a tall, dignified man with a look of deepest concern on his face rose from behind his desk out on the floor.

"Will the Senator yield to his distinguished colleague from Pennsylvania?"

Crane turned, scowling. "I will yield to no man on matters of grave import." With that he turned and continued with his revelations. "The people of this nation have been deprived of the knowledge that the invasion from space has already begun. A vanguard of hideous, half-human creatures have even now achieved a beach-head on our planet. Even now, the evil hordes from beyond the stars . . ."

The Vice-President looked around in a daze. Had someone forgotten to brief him? Had that project come to a head overnight? The last he'd heard there had been much doubt as to—

". . . The injustice perpetrated on the American people in this matter has been monstrous. And this is not because of any lack of knowledge on the part of the government. It has been because of the petty natures of the men to whom this secret has been entrusted. Jealousies have dictated policy where selfless public service was of the most vital importance . . ."

The floor was filling up. The visitor's gallery was wrapped in hushed silence. Newsmen, informed of sensational developments, were rushing down corridors.

And the Vice-President was wondering why he hadn't had the good sense to refuse the nomination.

". . . These invaders from another planet are not strangers to the men in power. It is on record that they are inhuman monsters capable of killing without mercy—yet they are quite ordinary in appearance. They walk the streets, unsuspected, among us. It is on record right here in Washington that these creatures are not human but, rather, soulless androids, manufactured to destroy us, by a race so far ahead of us in scientific knowledge that we are like children by comparison . . ."

"Will the Senator yield to the Senator from Alabama?"

"I will not. I refuse to be gagged in the process of acquainting the American people with facts upon which their very survival depends."

The floor was crowded now. The press and the visitors' galleries were packed as Senator Crane's words continued to boom forth.

And in the press gallery a reporter from the Sioux City *Clarion* looked at a representative of the London *Times*, and said, "Good God! He's gone off his rocker!"

The Englishman, aloof but definitely enthralled, touched his mustache delicately and answered, "Quite."

*****

Frank Corson rang the bell and waited at the door of Rhoda Kane's apartment. The door opened. She wore a pale blue brunch coat. Her hair glowed in the light of midmorning, but her face was pale and a little drawn.

Her eyes were slightly red, as though she might have been crying.

"Hello, Rhoda."

"Hello, Frank."

"I really didn't expect to find you. I was going to write a note and slip it under the door."

"I didn't feel well today so I didn't go to work."

"May I come in?"

"Of course."

Inside, a shadow of concern moved like a quick cloud across her beautiful face. "You don't look well, Frank."

"I'm quite all right, really. Haven't been sleeping too well, but there's been a lot on my mind."

"I've been hoping you'd phone."

"I wanted to but there didn't seem to be anything to say. Nothing except that I'm sorry I let you down so miserably."

"Frank! You didn't. You really didn't. It was just that—oh, it's not important any more."

"No. It's not important now."

"Would you like a drink?"

"Thanks, no. I've come to say good-bye."

"Good-bye?"

"Yes. I'm leaving Park Hill—leaving New York. I'm going into a small Minnesota hospital to finish my internship. Then I'll probably practice out there somewhere."

Behind the new glitter of her eyes there was stark misery. "Frank—Frank—what went wrong with us?"

The appeal was a labored whisper.

"I don't know, Rhoda. I should know but I don't. I should have known what was wrong so I could have done something about it. It just went sour, I guess."

She turned and walked to the window. He wondered if there were tears in her eyes.

"Good-bye, Rhoda."

"Good-bye, Frank. I'm sorry."

The door hadn't quite closed. Now, as Frank Corson turned, he found it open. A man stood there—a man in a blue suit with empty eyes.

Frank stared at the man for long seconds. His eyes went toward the window. Rhoda had turned. She was watching the man in the doorway, looking past Frank at the creature from somewhere in space who was neither man nor machine. *But how—?* Frank Corson asked himself the question. *Good God! How had this thing come about?*

"Not—not *him*," he finally exploded.

Rhoda was walking forward. The look of fevered excitement was in her eyes. "Please leave, Frank." She did not look at him as she spoke. She kept her eyes on the man in the blue suit.

"Not him!"

"Please leave, Frank."

But it was too late. The door had closed. The man was looking at Frank. "Sit down," he said.

Frank Corson sat down. He saw the man and he saw Rhoda, but they seemed unimportant. Something had happened to his mind and he was busy struggling with it. That was all that was important.

The strange lethargy that came like a cloud over his mind was beyond understanding.

*****

Captain Abrams looked into the closet and back at Brent Taber. His lips were back a little off his teeth. With Abrams, this indicated anger.

"All right. What does Washington do about this one? Does Washington tell us to be good little boys and go hand out parking tickets?"

"It wasn't like that," Taber said.

"It doesn't much matter how it was. The thing is—how is it going to be now?"

"You got a murder, friend. Plain and simple. What do the New York police do when they get a murder?"

Abrams spoke bitterly. "Sometimes they let a panel truck drive in and haul the body away and that's that."

"Let's save the sarcasm until later. I called you in. It's your case. What do you want me to do?"

"Talk a little, maybe. The other one—now this one. The same killer?"

"I think so."

"What does he look like?"

"Medium height. One-eighty. Around forty. And dangerous."

"Dangerous, he says," Abrams muttered. "Any idea where we might go to have a little talk with him?"

"No, can't say that I have."

"Try the streets of Manhattan—is that it?"

"I guess that's about it." Taber paused. "Wait a minute. If he's looking for a spot to hide in he wouldn't come back here and he certainly wouldn't try King's room. There's just a wide-open chance he might have another location. Wait a minute while I look up an address."

*****

An hour after he'd finished delivering his speech on the floor of the Senate, Crane held a press conference in one of Washington's most important hotels. The place was crowded. He stood on a platform, looked out over a sea of heads, and pointed at an upraised hand for the first question.

"Senator, have you gotten any reaction from the people of your state on the revelations contained in your speech?"

"There has been very little time, but telegrams have been pouring in."

"What is the reaction?"

"Frankly, I haven't had time to read them. However, I think there is little doubt as to the mood of my people. They will be indignant and angry at Washington bungling."

He pointed to another hand.

"Senator, granting the details you outlined are accurate, have you any knowledge as to—"

"Young man. *Every* detail I outlined was completely accurate." Senator Crane withered the reporter with a hostile look and pointed elsewhere.

"Senator, did you consult with the people responsible for handling the situation before making your speech?"

"I tried. I was willing to co-operate in every way, but my patience ran out. Also, I was alarmed at the bungling and inefficiency I saw. For that reason I went straight to the people with my story."

"Senator, I have a wire from the governor of your state. It just arrived in response to my query as to his attitude on this affair. The governor says, quote, *No comment*, unquote. Would *you* care to comment on his statement?"

Senator Crane thought he heard a faint ripple of mirth drift across the room. But, of course, he had to be mistaken. "I think the governor replied wisely. I expect to return home and confer with him as soon as possible."

"Senator, can you explain why, out of all the able, sincere officials in Washington, D.C., elected or otherwise, you were the only one with enough wisdom and courage to put this matter before the people?"

"Young man, I am not going to pass judgment on anyone in Washington or elsewhere. Each of us, I'm sure, does his duty as he sees it."

Again it seemed to Senator Crane that he heard a ripple of mirth—louder this time. It had to be something to do with the acoustics. Except that he was suddenly aware of smiles, too. The next question had to do with possible consultation with Russia on the matter of the coming space invasion.

Senator Crane agreed that such consultation should be made and then retired hastily into seclusion. A touch of panic hit him. He felt like a man who was far out in the water without a boat, with the closest land a few hundred feet straight down. Good God! Had he miscalculated? Of course not. He had only to await the verdict of the nation's top newspapers before proceeding with the publicity program that might well make him presidential timber.

*****

John Dennis, for the first time since Rhoda had known him, seemed nervous. He kept licking his lips and shifting his eyes from Rhoda to Frank Corson.

Frank Corson sat quietly, keeping his thoughts to himself.

Rhoda crossed to the liquor cabinet and poured a double Scotch. She went to the sofa and sat down a little uncertainly.

"I guess you two haven't met. John, this is Frank Corson."

John Dennis paid no attention. He walked to the sofa, sat down, and took a sheaf of notes from his jacket pocket.

"I've known Mr. Dennis for quite some time," Frank commented wryly.

"Be quiet."

John Dennis' tone was neither hostile nor friendly. They were the words of a person whose mind was on other things. They watched him as his eyes scanned the notes.

He appeared to be memorizing them.

The air became somewhat electric, the silence so deep it seemed to scream. Rhoda looked across at Frank Corson. Frank's expression was empty, as though he'd suffered some traumatic emotional blow and was struggling to recover.

John Dennis stirred. He also appeared to be struggling. He turned his eyes on the drink Rhoda was holding. He took it out of her hand and downed it in a single gulp.

They watched as he went back to work, leafing through the notes, one at a time. As he came close to the end, he lifted his head and shook it violently, as though from sudden pain. He scowled at the empty glass he'd handed back to Rhoda.

"Do you want another?" she inquired.

"Give me another."

She poured a second Scotch and handed it to him. He drank it like so much water.

The last sheet of notations was covered. Then John Dennis sat motionless for a minute, his frown and uncertainty returning. "It's hard to project the details," he said. "All this detail. Difficult."

He dropped the last sheet and got up and poured himself another Scotch. "They will make an army now," he said. The Scotch went down smoothly. He went to the window and looked out. "This planet is different. The sun there is blue and the air is very thin. Their bodies are nothing, but their heads are very big. Now they will create an army and take this planet."

Frank Corson was shaking his head slowly like a groggy fighter. Rhoda sat huddled on the sofa, her mind such a mixture of tumbling emotions that it seemed to be trying to tear itself out of her head. John Dennis came back and stood in the middle of the room. He swayed drunkenly. "So many things I don't understand.

I see people I know—or I should know. I—" He turned his eyes—eyes no longer empty—on Rhoda.

"I want to make love!"

Frank Corson got up from his chair and hurled himself on Dennis.

Rhoda screamed.

*****

Senator Crane sat at his desk. There were a pile of newspapers in front of him. The first one carried a front page story with the headline:

SENATOR CRANE WARNS OF SPACE INVASION

Shades of Orson Wells' Martian
Scare Stalks Capitol Corridors.

Crane tossed the paper aside listlessly and picked up the second one:

SENATORS VOICE CONCERN FOR
SANITY OF COLLEAGUE

Crane in Stunning Tirade
Warns of Science-Fiction Disaster.

The third paper featured an internationally syndicated columnist, famous for his biting wit:

*****

Senator Crane today launched a one-man campaign to make America space-conscious. If there was any Madison Avenue thinking behind the launching it was certainly lower Madison Avenue.

In order to make his point—exactly what this was confused a vast roomful of newspapermen—the Senator invented a race of creatures called androids. These androids, it seems, look exactly like Tom Smith down the block except that they'd just as soon cut your throat as not.

We fear the Senator must have been watching the wrong television shows—knives yet, ugh!—possibly *Jim Bowie*, because there wasn't a ray gun nor a disintegrator in his whole bag of exhibits.

All in all, it would appear that the project was pointed toward making the people Senator Crane-conscious rather than aiming their attention at the deadly heavens.

*****

Senator Crane put that paper aside and looked at the next. This one, more so than all the rest, was completely factual:

SENATOR CRANE DELUGED
WITH WIRES FROM HOME
Constituents Claim Washington Ridicule
Heaped on Senator Reflects Against State.

Crane dropped the paper and got up from the desk. That son-of-a-bitch Taber was to blame for this. Shaping up a goddamn hoax and feeding it out piecemeal. By God—!

He went to the desk and dialed, and when the answer came he said, "Halliday? Senator Crane here. I want to have a little talk with you about that damned tape. It's pretty obvious now that Taber planted it in a deliberate attempt to . . . What's that? An appointment! Why, goddamn it, who the hell do you think you are? . . . Fifteen minutes next Wednesday? You're talking to a United States Senator—"

But Crane was no longer talking to Halliday. He had hung up.

Crane dialed another number. A pleasant female voice said, "Matthew Porter's office."

"This is Senator Crane. Put Porter on."

"Just a moment."

Crane waited. He waited for what seemed like ages, but a glance at his watch told him it had been less than five minutes. He disconnected and dialed again.

"This is Crane. We got cut off. I want to talk to Porter."

"I'm sorry but Mr. Porter has gone for the day."

"Well, where can I reach him? It's important."

"I'm sorry. Mr. Porter left no number."

"When will he be back?"

"He didn't say."

Crane slammed the phone down. "The bastards!" he snarled. "The lousy, crummy bastards. Running like a pack of scared rats. Bureaucrats! Damned, cowardly, self-appointed opportunists!"

He stopped cursing and sat for a while.

When he got up and left the office he looked and felt old but he had faced a truth. It would not be necessary to campaign next year.

It wouldn't be of any use.

13

John Dennis showed human surprise as Frank Corson lunged at him. He had either been lax in using the controlling power he'd been given, or else Frank Corson had an exceptional resistance.

Dennis released Rhoda, swayed drunkenly under Frank Corson's clumsy football-type tackle, and swung his arm like a pivoting beam. The blow was a lucky one. His fist smashed low on Corson's jaw, numbing the nerves of his neck on the left side.

Corson went down and, as he lay helpless, Dennis kicked him twice—once in the side and once, viciously effectively, in the head. Corson rolled over and lay still.

Dennis looked down at him in a drunken daze. "They will make an army and bring it here."

Rhoda, standing in the center of an emotional maelstrom, watched the struggle from the prison of her own horror. At that moment she was physically, mentally and spiritually ill; a human being caught in the midst of forces beyond her knowledge and control.

Dennis laid a heavy hand on her shoulder. "I want to make love."

"No—no. Please—"

The drunkenness ebbed slightly and his eyes emptied. They looked into Rhoda's. She shivered. He took the neck of her brunch coat in his fist and jerked downward. She had just come from the shower when she'd first opened the door for Frank Corson, and the vicious denuding gesture left her completely naked.

Dennis went clumsily to his knees, his arms around her, and he pulled her to the floor. She sobbed, but the tears were gone now and they were dry, wracking sobs.

"Undress me."

She fumbled with his jacket and pulled it off while he knelt there in anticipation of he knew not what; wondering, wanting, knowing only an urge he could not understand but which had become a compulsion.

She took off his necktie and unbuttoned his shirt. Frank Corson stirred but did not regain consciousness. "Please," Rhoda said, "let me help him."

In answer, Dennis put his arms around her and drew her to him. "We will make love."

"Yes—yes, we will make love—"

The ring of the doorbell was like thunder in the room. Dennis tensed, his eyes widened, and he got to his feet and stood swaying. Looking up at him, Rhoda saw a trapped animal, but the excitement was still there and she wanted to take him in her arms and hold him and protect him from the world.

But he had forgotten her. A cunning sneer took the place of the slavering animal look and he ran to the kitchen to reappear moments later with a butcher knife in his hand.

The bell rang again. Dennis snarled at the door and, in some kind of sheer ecstatic bravado, emitted a Tarzan roar.

Instantly a weight hit the door from the outside. It shuddered but did not give. Dennis crouched, gripping his knife. Frank Corson staggered to his feet and hurled himself groggily at the android. Dennis roared again, pushed away and arced the knife at his throat.

Rhoda screamed and lunged at Dennis' legs. "No! No! Stop it! Please!"

Dennis teetered under her weight and the knife slanted downward across Frank's chest. It ripped a red gash as the door shuddered a third time.

Dennis turned in that direction and crouched. The door splintered and flew open. Dennis lunged, like a line-bucking football player. He hit both Brent Taber and Captain Abrams simultaneously, sprawling them both and sending Abrams' gun spinning out of his hand.

He leaped over them and dashed down the hall where the elevator man waited uncertainly, not sure whether to dispute the right of way or not. His indecision was fatal. Dennis wrapped an arm around his neck, pulled his head back and cut his throat with one slash of the knife.

Captain Abrams' head had hit a doorjamb opposite the entrance to Rhoda's apartment. He stirred and tried to come erect but he was unable to make it.

Brent Taber clawed the gun off the floor and came to one knee. He got off one shot as the elevator door was closing and saw the android spin away from the controls as the impact of the slug smashed the bone of his shoulder.

Taber lunged to his feet and went for the stairs.

There was no one in the lobby when he arrived there—no dead bodies, either. But on the sidewalk, in front of the building, a woman lay dead in a pool of blood.

In a sick rage, Taber looked in both directions and saw the android dive through a group of people half a block away. He tipped them over like tenpins and ran on. Taber gripped the gun tight and started in pursuit.

He could not fire because there was enough sidewalk traffic to make it dangerous. On ahead, the android's path was blocked by a man. He sought to get clear but the android passed him close enough to jam the knife into his neck and send him screaming to the sidewalk.

A uniformed patrolman appeared on the other side of the street, further down. He took the situation in and understood Taber's frantic gesture. A car screamed to a halt as the patrolman raced across the street, drawing his gun.

The android, seeing his escape cut off, veered into an areaway. The patrolman got there first and plunged in after him.

Taber, gasps tearing at his lungs, arrived thirty seconds later. During that time, he'd expected the sound of shots from the patrolman's gun. But there was silence.

He braked on his heels, skidded into the areaway, and saw the android advancing on the patrolman. The latter stood motionless, the gun hanging useless at his side.

"Drop! Drop!" Taber yelled. He cursed as he tried to angle in the narrow areaway in order to get a clear shot.

The android advanced with his knife raised. In desperation, Taber fired at the lethal fist that held the weapon. And he was lucky. The hand snapped open under the ripping impact of the bullet and the knife rang sharply against the wall as it ricocheted to the ground.

Only then, did the patrolman obey the order to drop. He went to one knee and Brent Taber fired three shots into the chest of the android.

He hesitated. There was only one slug left in the revolver. If the three didn't spot the android, he planned to wait for closer contact and put the sixth slug into the forehead.

The android shuddered. The fire and frenzy went out of him. He tried to lift a leg and was surprised when it didn't move. He looked down at it. Completely bemused, he peered down at his crimson chest. He looked up at Taber without anger, only with surprise. A distinct expression of wistful regret crossed his face as he sank to the ground.

The tenth android was dead.

The patrolman came shakily to his feet. His face was as pale as death. "I—I don't know what happened. Buck fever. Pure buck fever, and I've been on the force for ten years."

"Don't worry about it," Taber said.

"Don't *worry*. All of a sudden I freeze under pressure and he says, 'Don't worry.'"

"I meant it. This is no ordinary man. It wasn't buck fever at all. I couldn't have faced him myself if I hadn't rattled him with that lucky shot."

The patrolman wanted to believe. He most pathetically wanted to believe. "Honest?"

"It's the God's honest truth. No man could have stood in front of that killer and pulled a trigger. He's a master hypnotist. You're all right. We won't say a word about what happened in here. And you'll have no trouble in the future."

The patrolman shook his head. "Still, I gotta do something about it."

"Talk to your psychiatrist," Taber said. "In the meantime, keep that crowd out there from spilling in here."

Taber pushed out through the choked entrance to the areaway and went back up the street. It was alive with activity now and he passed unnoticed. No one recognized him as the man who had given chase in the bloody business that would make headlines that evening in every New York newspaper.

And yet the radio and TV news commentators gave it no special attention. It went in along with other items of the day's news as a more or less routine big-city happening.

One national-hookup headliner stated: "In New York City today, a man identified as John Dennis, address unknown, went berserk in a fashionable Upper East Side apartment. Dennis, wielding a knife, killed a man and a woman, and seriously wounded another man before he was cut down by police bullets.

"A jet airliner, down in the North Atlantic today, imperiled the lives of seventy-six . . ."

*****

Frank Corson lay propped on two pillows in a private room of the Park Hill Hospital. Rhoda Kane sat in a chair beside the bed. She was pale and very beautiful. The fire was now gone from her body and the fever from her eyes.

"They say he wasn't human. They say he was an android." She

shuddered, looked down quickly, then slowly raised her head.

"Yes."

"I'll—I'll never understand. I get sick thinking about it. I'll just never understand."

"He was human and yet not human. He had extraordinary powers that we don't begin to understand, so that what happened to you is no disgrace."

"It's a terrible disgrace."

"It happened to me, too. When he told me to sit down I had to do it. I was helpless."

"But you fought! You overcame it."

Frank Corson smiled wryly. "No, I didn't. It was just that he'd had little time to work on me. It was a single mental blow, so to speak, that laid me out. Like one punch in the ring. Gradually, I came out of it."

"I think I *tried* to fight."

"Of course, you did. The disgrace was mine. I acted like a child. I should have realized that something extraordinary had happened. But I nursed my miserable little ego like a three-year-old."

"How could you know? My cruelty to you—"

"Don't talk like that! I knew about the ninth android, and I met the tenth one in front of your apartment that second morning. I should have associated. Brent Taber did, otherwise we might both be dead."

"It's all over now. It doesn't make any difference."

"No, it doesn't make any difference."

She looked at him in silence for several moments. "You've changed, Frank."

"Yes, I guess I have. I guess we all grow up eventually. We all face reality and live with it."

"Frank—I think I'm going to cry."

He could not turn his eyes in her direction. He looked straight ahead but his voice was soft. "Go ahead, Rhoda. I understand."

They were silent for a time, then Rhoda began to cry quietly into her handkerchief. After a while even that sound was stilled.

He turned to look at her. She was standing beside the bed. He almost reached out and took her hand, but drew his own back at the last minute.

"How soon will you be leaving?" she asked.

"The wound was superficial. I really didn't need to be hospitalized. I'm being released tomorrow morning. I'll probably leave immediately."

"You'll make a fine doctor, Frank."

"Thank you, I'll try."

"Good-bye, Frank."

"Good-bye—darling."

She turned and fled.

And judging by the deep sadness in his soul, he knew he had hit bottom.

There was no place to go but up.

*****

Brent Taber's phone rang.

"Hello, Taber. Halliday here."

"How are you, Halliday."

"Tops, old man. Ragged by the stress of it all, of course, but tops."

Taber waited. Halliday waited. Seeing that he would get no help, he said, "By the way, that little . . . misunderstanding we had, the Senator Crane thing, I'm sure you realized that our talk was . . . well, the words were put into my mouth. I felt the same way about the oaf as you did. But sometimes, in the line of duty, old man . . . well, I know you were reading between my lines all the time."

"I'm pretty good at that."

"I knew we understood each other."

"Is that what you called about?"

"Yes, but I've got a little tip for you. They want to see you upstairs. I happen to know they liked the way things turned out. Just between you and me, the humiliation of Crane made certain high officials pretty happy. I was queried and I gave you all the credit."

"Before or after the good Senator fell on his face?"

Halliday laughed. "Okay, pal. You're entitled to your little dig. But you know this—I'm with you and I always will be."

"And I'm with you, too, pal," Brent said wearily and hung up.

The phone rang again. Automatically, Brent picked up the receiver.

"Brent? Porter on this end. How is it with you, old man?"

"Ducky. Just ducky."

Porter laughed. "Just called to say, 'Good job well done.'"

"Thanks."

"Want to give you a little tip, too. They want you upstairs. A commendation. Not generally known, though. And you deserve it. You'll be called up tomorrow."

"You never know the day or the hour."

The laugh came again. "You're humor is priceless, old man."

"Isn't it?"

"Another thing—I got pretty hot when I got wind of how the ground was being cut out from under you. I made it my business to do something about it. I hate to see a good man pushed around. Of course I okayed the orders cutting you down—a matter of routine—I had to follow through. But then I got busy. A thing like that won't happen again."

"Thanks, Porter. It warms a man to know he's got a friend—a friend like you."

"Just between us, old man, I'm one of your admirers." Porter laughed and sprayed charm through the phone like perfume from an atomizer. "But if you quote me, I'll deny it."

"Oh, I wouldn't think of quoting you, old man," Taber replied in a kindly voice and put down the phone.

He sat back and closed his eyes. Three people dead. One person maimed. Blood in the streets.

Good job well done.

He opened a drawer of his desk and reached for the Scotch bottle.

*****

At the Newark Airport he would not trust his suitcase to a porter because the leather loop holding one side of the handle was very thin and he was afraid it would break.

Once he had been ashamed of the shabbiness of the bag and had planned to buy a new one, but now there was an affinity between them, a kind of warmth.

Were they companions in misery?

He asked the question with a quick smile and then realized he was not miserable. A little bleak of mind, perhaps, with Minnesota and what lay ahead affording no glow of anticipation in his mind. But that would pass. No, he had relegated the hurt to a mental pigeonhole; maybe he would bring it out and look at it once in a while, after enough time had passed.

But he was not miserable.

He went to the counter, checked in, and they told him his plane would take off on time. He glanced at his watch. Thirty-two minutes.

He went back to the bench and found Rhoda Kane sitting beside his suitcase.

She wore a plain, black suit with a ridiculous little black hat and she was so beautiful he was angry with her. He hated her. This good-bye wasn't necessary. Why had she come?

Her face was pale and drawn; her smile was as abstract as the mystery on the lips of the Mona Lisa. She laid a hand on the suitcase.

"We had our first quarrel over it, remember? We went to Puerto Rico for that week and I wanted to use mine but you said, 'Goddamn it, if you're ashamed of my suitcase you're ashamed of me, so the hell with it.'"

"I remember."

He sat down beside her, lit a cigarette, and then dropped it on the floor and stepped on it. They both looked straight ahead.

"Take me with you, Frank."

"That's impossible."

"I know, but take me with you."

"There will be no money. I'll live in a stuffy room somewhere."

"What difference does that make? Take me."

"You have your job. You're on the way up. It would be unthinkable."

"I don't have any job. I quit. I was halfway through a piece of copy—very important copy—and I got up and walked into Mr. Frankel's office. I said, 'Mr. Frankel, it's been very nice working for you. I appreciate all you've done but I'm leaving now. The pencils are all sharpened on my desk and the next girl can have the new leather-bound address book in the lower right hand drawer that I bought but never used! That was a silly thing to say, wasn't it?"

"I suppose so."

"And the way I phrased it. I actually said I'd bought the lower right hand drawer and hadn't used it—take me with you, Frank."

"Rhoda, I was so wrong in—"

"*I* was wrong, Frank. I was trying to mold you into my way of life. I wanted you, but only as a part of my own eager little world. I had money so I furnished my apartment. I put this here and that there, and hung a toothbrush over the sink as necessarily functional, and then I decided I needed a man in the same way and so I picked you.

"But I found out that the man in the bed was the most important part of it and without him there wasn't anything. Without him I didn't want any of the other. Now . . . I want to be a wife. A wife is a person who goes where her husband goes and lives where he lives and shares what he has. You don't barter and trade—this for that—give up this part to get that. You give up everything and yet it isn't like that at all because you're really getting everything."

He took out another cigarette.

"Oh, Frank, it's all mixed up and I'm going to cry, I think."

"It's not mixed up at all," he said quietly. He turned to look at her, half frowning, half smiling. "Now why in the hell couldn't you have given me a little notice? Twenty minutes to plane time and I've got to get another reservation."

"I'm sorry, Frank."

"Maybe there isn't a seat."

"Wouldn't that be terrible?"

"Then we'll have to wait over."

"Why don't you go and see?"

Five minutes later they were walking down the west tunnel to gate twenty-six.

Frank Corson grinned. "Come on, woman, I'm going to take you across state lines for immoral purposes."

"How wonderful," she breathed.

*****

Brent Taber was human and his triumph had been a thing of satisfaction to him—but only momentarily. Now it had a slightly sour taste.

Not that he was unhappy. He was content and almost relaxed as he sat in Doctor Entman's patio and worked on a Scotch and soda.

"A nice night," Entman said.

"Beautiful. Those stars are about ready to fall into our laps."

"Menace out there? It seems unthinkable."

"Doesn't it?"

"The human animal is a strange creature. He's so capable of refusing to believe what he doesn't want to believe."

"Maybe he's smarter than we think. Maybe there's no point in looking at a pending disaster from every angle. The what-will-be-will-be attitude isn't necessarily like that of the ostrich which sticks its head in the sand."

"Do the people inside really believe?" Entman asked.

"It's pretty difficult to tell. Sometimes I wonder what my own real feelings are."

"I wasn't completely briefed on how it ended," Entman said delicately.

"I think the phony specifications got through."

"If they did—if things are really as they appear—"

Taber smiled in the darkness. "Are *you* beginning to doubt, Doctor?"

"Oh, be quiet," Entman said with friendly petulance. "I was going to say that I was rather proud of those details. If our hostiles out there follow my specifications, they'll create androids with much smaller lungs and non-porous skin that will give them no end of trouble when they start chasing frightened householders down the streets of the world."

Taber chuckled. "I remember a story about the Japanese Navy. They were supposed to have built some ships to specifications stolen in England. When launched, they slid out into the bay and tipped over."

Entman sighed. "I wish I could get some of the data those creatures used in the construction of the androids."

"You'd like to make one of your own?"

"It would solve the servant problem. Terrible here in Washington."

"Labor unions would holler bloody murder."

"You can't stop progress."

Suddenly Entman got to his feet. He walked to the edge of the patio and looked upward. Taber saw his face in the light streaming from the living room—he seemed frightened.

"Brent! It's such a helpless feeling. What do we do?"

Brent Taber got up and went over and stood beside Entman. He, too, looked up into the velvet night; the beautiful, quiet, impersonal night.

The sinister night.

"We watch the stars," Brent said. "And we wait."

THE END

www.ingramcontent.com/pod-product-compliance
Lightning Source LLC
Chambersburg PA
CBHW031840170626
46807CB00004B/1540